The Hollow Ones

The Hollow Ones

저자 박태성

하움

01

Chapter

✦

The world is not on my side

The world is not on my side.

Our family decided to move because of my dad's work. No warning, no chance to plead. Just a cardboard box and a deadline. Each step toward the new beginning felt like dragging a heavy chain behind me—one link for every friend, every inside joke, every late-night walk under the dim streetlights of my old neighborhood.

My parents acted like it was no big deal. "You'll make new friends," they said. But I couldn't just wipe the slate clean and pretend the past didn't exist. I didn't want a new beginning. I wanted my life back.

Room by room, our house was hollowing out. One by one, the things that made it ours disappeared. My posters, gone. My books, packed. The sound of familiar laughter echoed less and less.

There was one spot I couldn't ignore, though.

In the corner of the living room, near the window, the wooden floor had a dull, faded patch, worn smooth over time. The paint had chipped and peeled, and it was cooler than the rest of the room. But to Caramel, it was his spot. Every afternoon, when I came home from school, I'd find him curled up there, soaking in the sunlight. He'd lift his head for a second when he heard the door, tail thumping slowly, then drift back into his nap.

Sometimes he'd snore. Sometimes he'd twitch, his legs kicking in dreamland. I used to wonder what he dreamed about. Running through fields? Chasing something? Or just lying there in the sun, warm and safe?

He will always be in my heart.

When I got in the car, I sat by the window and didn't say a word. As we drove through my old neighborhood, every familiar sight twisted my chest tighter—the market on the corner, the old playground with the squeaky swing, even the crooked sign at the pet store where we first picked up Caramel as a puppy.

I didn't cry. But something inside me stayed heavy.

At the airport, I kept my eyes low. I didn't want to see my parent's fake cheerfulness. I didn't want to cry in front of strangers. So I shut it all down. I boarded the plane like I was stepping into a dream someone else was having.

The new place was... okay. Small school, quiet streets, a big lake nearby. Dad and I went fishing on weekends. I didn't say much, but he seemed glad we had something to do together.

Then I met James.

He's kind of ridiculous, honestly. Always joking, always making up stories. He once told me he saw a fish the size of a car in the lake. Then he laughed and said, "Or maybe it was a log. But a very suspicious log." Sometimes he gets weirdly serious, though, and his smile vanishes like a light switching off. But that's rare. Most of the time, he's just... good to be around.

One day, he invited me to his house after school. We dropped our bags and started playing an old horror game—one of those glitchy ones with jump scares that you still fall for, even when you know they're coming.

Right after one of those jumps, James turned to me with that grin of his.

"You know this school's cursed, right?"

I raised an eyebrow. "What?"

He nodded. "Dead serious. They say a student disappeared here, like, ten years ago. Poof. Never found. Some people say... he's still in the school."

I rolled my eyes. "Let me guess—he turned into a ghost and hunts you?"

James gave me a long look, then shrugged. "Maybe. I dunno.

But people hear things. Walls creaking. Voices. Scratches. You'll see."

I laughed it off.

I thought he was just messing around.

But now... I'm not so sure.

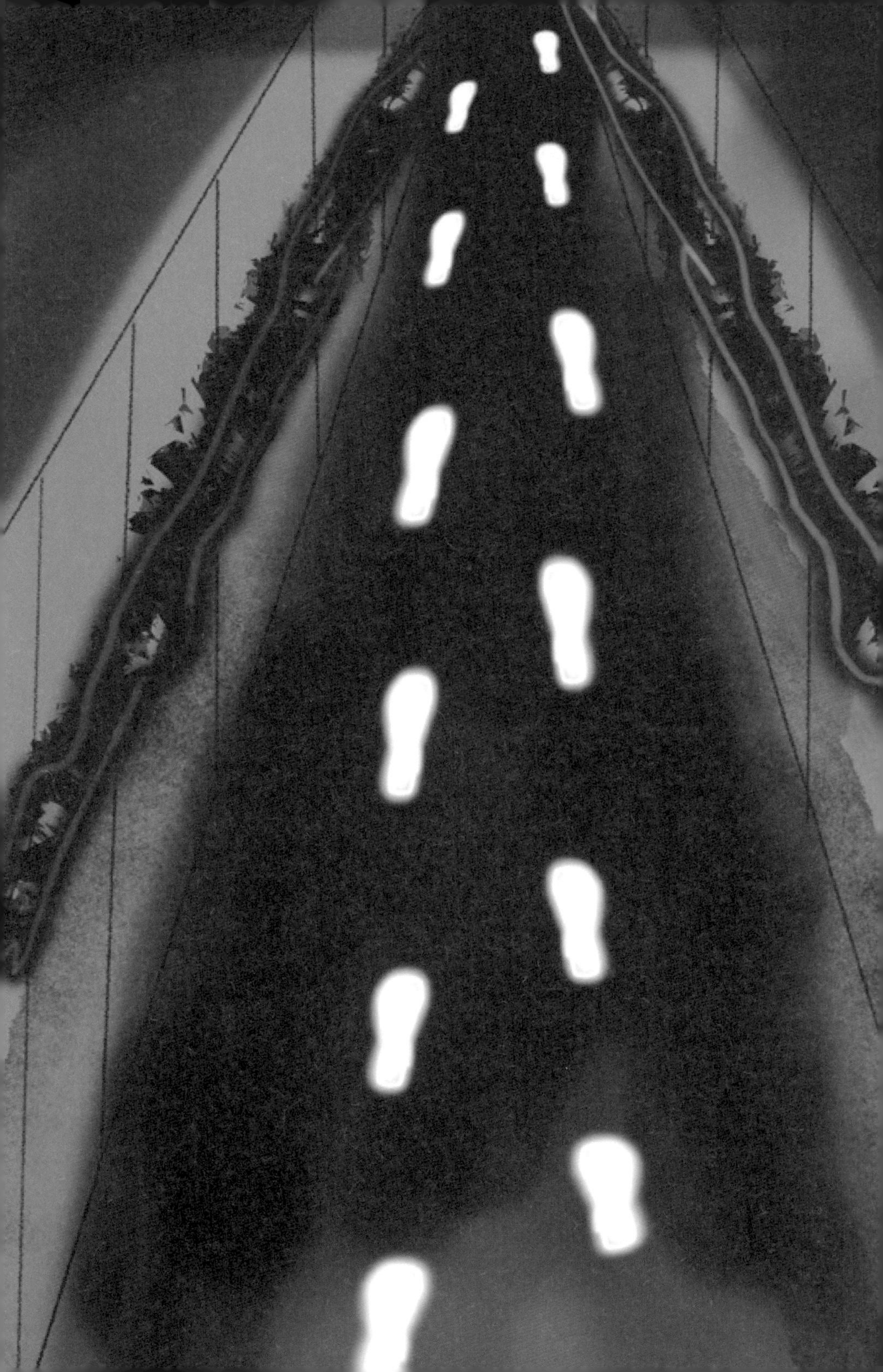

02
Chapter

✦

The First Sign

It started with a fight.

I didn't mean for it to happen. Honestly, I'm not even the kind of person who gets in trouble. But when someone says something about your family—especially when they don't know anything—you don't always think straight.

His name was Derek. He's one of those guys who thinks he's funnier than he actually is, always mouthing off, always pushing people's buttons. He made some dumb joke about my dad, something about us moving because we "ran out of money." I tried to let it go. I really did.

But then he said something about Caramel. I don't even know how he knew. Maybe James mentioned it once. Maybe I did. But he said, "You should've left that mutt behind sooner. Guess even dogs know when to quit."

Violent red

Next thing I knew, I was on top of him, fists clenched, yelling something I can't even remember. A teacher pulled me off. Derek had a bloody lip and a smug grin like he got exactly what he wanted.

I got detention.

The halls were different after hours. A lecture. And a requirement to finish my homework alone after school that day.

Gone was the usual rush of footsteps, the slam of lockers, the hum of a hundred conversations. The silence wasn't peaceful—it was hollow, like the building was holding its breath. The overhead lights buzzed faintly, flickering once or twice as I walked past rows of classroom doors. Every sound felt amplified. My own footsteps. The creak of the floor. Even the zipper on my backpack seemed too loud.

I made my way to my locker to grab my workbook.

That's when I saw it.

Deep. Ugly. Fresh. Carved into the back wall of the locker like someone had jammed a knife in and dragged it downward. The wood underneath was raw, splintered. I stared at it for a long moment. I hadn't noticed it before, and I would've noticed something like that.

Then I heard it.

A whisper.

Not loud. Not clear. But it was there. Breathy. Garbled. Like someone was behind the locker... or in the wall beside it.

I froze.

My brain told me it was the wind. Maybe the air system is kicking in. But my gut knew better. It wasn't a breeze. It wasn't mechanical.

It was a voice.

I spun around. No one. The hall was empty. I backed away from my locker, heart thumping like a drumbeat.

I grabbed my book and slammed the locker shut, the sound echoing down the hall like a gunshot. I didn't wait. I walked fast. Almost ran.

That night, I messaged James.

me: there's something in the school
james: oh no u found the ghost lol
me: I'm serious. there was a scratch in my locker. and a whisper. no joke
james: what'd it say?
me: I couldnt tell. but it was real
james: maybe the missing kid wanted your geometry notes

He was joking. Of course he was. But I couldn't even smile.

At lunch the next day, I told John, Will, and Mike.

They listened politely. But the way their eyes darted to one another said everything.

"It's probably just old vents," Will said.

"Yeah," John added. "Or some idiot messing around. Derek's friends, maybe."

Mike just shook his head. "You've had a rough week. Don't let your brain trick you."

I didn't argue.

Later that day, I peeked into my locker again.

The scratch was still there. But this time, I noticed something else.

A faint smear—like a handprint. Only the fingers were too long.

Boneless. Smudged across the metal like something had dragged itself along the surface.

That night, sleep didn't come easy.

I laid in bed staring at the ceiling. The shadows in the corners of my room seemed darker than usual. I kept my lamp on, telling myself it was just for comfort—but in truth, I was afraid to turn it off. My window was closed, but I swore I could hear something faint, like distant whispering, carried through the walls.

It couldn't be real.

I told myself it was just stress. Just leftover adrenaline from the fight. But every time I closed my eyes, I saw that scratch. Heard that whisper. Felt that cold weight behind me in the hallway.

At some point, I turned onto my side and pulled the blanket up tight around me, like I used to when I was a kid.

That's when I remembered Caramel.

He used to sleep on the floor beside my bed. Every night. The soft sound of his breathing always made me feel safe. But now that space was empty. Cold. And I felt like I wasn't alone anymore—but not in the comforting way.

More like something was watching me. Waiting.

And even with the lamp on, the dark still found a way to crawl in.

03

Chapter

✦

Library

I tried to forget.

About the whisper, the locker scratch, the handprint that didn't belong. I told myself it was just the stress of moving. The fight. The loneliness. My mind making things up to fill the gaps.

And for a while, it worked.

I went back to classes. Sat through lectures. Laughed when James cracked his usual weird jokes. Pretended everything was fine.

It wasn't, of course. But pretending is easier than explaining why you sleep with the lamp on every night.

It was a cloudy Saturday when I ended up at the library.

I hadn't planned on going. I never go there, actually. Too quiet. Too dusty. And it always felt like a place frozen in time, like the air had been sitting still for years. But that morning, something pushed me. Not a voice. Not a feeling I could explain. Just... a nudge. Like a hand on my shoulder, turning me toward the door.

So I walked.

The library sat on the corner of Maple and 3rd, an old brick building with ivy climbing up the side and a creaky green door. A bronze plaque near the entrance read: Westbridge Public Library - Est. 1902.

Inside, it smelled like old paper and floor wax. The lighting was dim, and every step I took echoed through the aisles. I nodded at the front desk lady, who didn't look up from her crossword, and wandered past rows of sagging shelves.

I wasn't sure what I was looking for.

At first, I pulled out a science book. Something about biology. Tried to study for the upcoming exam. But the words blurred together. Nothing stuck. My mind kept drifting.

So I stood up and walked. No plan, just moving.

Eventually, I found myself in a far corner of the library I'd never seen before. The Local History section.

The books here were different—older, heavier, with cracked leather spines and gold-embossed titles. I ran a finger along them absently, until one caught my eye:

"The History of Westbridge: Schools, Streets, and Secrets."

The last word made me pause.

Secrets?

I pulled the book from the shelf. It was thick. Probably a hundred years of boring town trivia, but I carried it back to my table anyway. When I opened it, the pages crackled softly, like they were whispering.

The early chapters were about the town's founders, the original settlers, some ancient land disputes. Then came the schools.

That's when I saw it: a section on Westbridge Middle School.

I leaned in.

It talked about the school being built in 1956. Described its red brick walls, the wide hallways, and the gym that doubled as an auditorium. And then, casually, it mentioned the pool.

The school featured a standard-sized indoor pool, installed in 1962...

Wait.

What pool?

I frowned. I've been at Westbridge for months now. I've seen every hallway. Every door. There's no pool.

I turned the page. Page 135... 136...

Then stopped.

Something felt off.

Page 137 started mid-sentence. A completely different topic. Like someone had yanked something out. The paper wasn't torn, but the tone shifted, the timeline jumped. It was like reading a story with a missing paragraph—no, more than that. A missing truth.

I flipped back. Then forward again.

136... then 137. No 136 and a half. No fold. Just... absence.

A cold prickle danced down my spine.

I looked around the library. It was silent. Still. The kind of quiet that feels unnatural, like the room is holding its breath again.

I read the section again, slowly this time.

The school featured a standard-sized indoor pool, installed in 1962, after a series of...

That's where the sentence ended. The next line was about fire drills in the 1970s. Nothing about the pool again. No mention of what the "series of" was.

A series of what?

Accidents? Complaints? Disappearances?

The more I stared at the page, the more my skin crawled.

I tried searching online on my phone, but there was barely anything. Just surface-level stuff. No mention of a pool. No blueprints. No photos.

That's when I realized—no one ever talks about it.

Not students. Not teachers. Not even on the school website.

I closed the book and shoved it back into the shelf harder than I meant to. Dust flew out. Something in the air shifted again—cold, subtle, sharp like the moment before a storm breaks.

As I walked out of the library, the front desk lady finally looked up. Her eyes flicked toward the book section I came from. Then back at me.

"You find what you were looking for?" she asked.

I shook my head.

"I don't know yet."

But I did know one thing.

Whatever was happening at Westbridge... it started a long time ago.

And someone didn't want it to be found.

As I turned to leave the library, the book still on my mind, a voice stopped me.

"Looking for something spooky?"

I blinked. The woman at the front desk had finally looked up from her crossword puzzle. Her glasses sat low on her nose, and her hair was swept back in a tight silver bun. There was something warm about her voice, but something sharp in her eyes—like she didn't miss much.

"I guess," I said, my voice a little hoarse from hours of silence.

She smiled and tapped her pen on the desk. "You're not the first kid to dig into that old thing. The History of Westbridge. Boring title, but people seem to think it hides all the town's secrets."

I hesitated. "Have you read it?"

She chuckled. "Read it? I could probably quote half of it. I went to Westbridge Middle myself. Long time ago, of course."

That made me pause. I stepped a little closer. "Really?"

"Mmhmm." She leaned back in her chair, stretching slightly. "Graduated before they built the new wing. Back when the cafeteria still had those orange plastic chairs that squeaked whenever you moved."

She glanced down at the book in my hands and tilted her head.

“Page 136?” she asked casually.

My fingers tightened around the cover. “Yeah. Did you notice that too?”

The woman didn’t answer right away. Her smile faded slightly. She folded her hands neatly in front of her.

“They say there was a printing error,” she said. “Something about a page being skipped in some early copies.”

“But this isn’t an early copy,” I replied. “It’s a newer reprint. And it still skips.”

She looked at me again. This time, her gaze was steadier, heavier.

“You found the part about the pool, didn’t you?”

I nodded slowly.

Her voice dropped slightly. “Most people don’t notice that section. Or they skim past it. You know why?”

I didn't speak. I just waited.

"Because that pool was sealed off," she said. "Not long after it opened. Officially, it was due to structural problems—leaks, cracked tiles, faulty drainage. But anyone who grew up here knows there was more to it."

A chill slid across the back of my neck. "What happened?"

She hesitated, then stood up slowly. Her knees cracked faintly as she moved from behind the desk and came around to stand beside me. Her voice softened, as if she didn't want others—or something else—to overhear.

"There was an incident," she said. "A long time ago. People whispered about it, but no one ever really knew what was true. The school paper never ran the story. The town paper didn't either. But when I was in seventh grade, there was a boy—quiet type. Kept to himself. I don't remember his name now."

She looked down for a moment, like she was searching her memory.

"He went missing," she continued. "One day he was there, next he was gone. Some said he ran away. Others said he drowned. But here's the strange part—no one ever found him. No body. No belongings. Just... disappeared."

"In the pool?" I asked, my voice barely above a whisper.

She nodded. "That's what people thought. That he was in the pool when it happened. Some of us even believed he was still in there, sealed up when they locked the basement level."

I stared at her. "Basement level? My school doesn't have a basement."

Her expression darkened slightly.

"Oh, it does," she said. "They just don't talk about it. The entrance was down near the old maintenance wing, past the custodial closet. Used to be a stairwell behind a steel door. They welded it shut when I was in eighth grade. After that... it was like it never existed."

I felt the air shift in my chest, a weight pressing down.

"Why don't people remember?" I asked. "Why isn't there anything about it online? No news articles, no yearbook photos, no blueprints. Nothing."

She shook her head, stepping back behind the desk.

"Some things," she said, "get buried. Sometimes on purpose."

I stood there, staring at her.

"You said you don't remember his name," I said. "But do you remember anything else about him?"

She looked at me for a long time. Then she reached into the drawer beside her and pulled out a worn index card.

"I don't know if this helps," she said. "But I wrote this down years ago, after hearing one of the janitors talk about it. Just a note to myself."

She handed it to me.

It read:

"Basement door welded shut. Pool drained, but one locker left open. Room always cold. Name might've been Eric or Evan. Avoid east hallway after dark."

My fingers trembled slightly as I folded the card and slid it into my pocket.

I didn't know what I was feeling—fear, curiosity, maybe both. But I knew one thing for sure.

Whatever happened in that school wasn't just a story.

And it wasn't over.

04
Chapter

✦

Voices in the Walls

It started again with a whisper.

Not loud. Not sudden. But clear.

I had been trying to forget about the library lady's words. About the missing boy. About the sealed pool no one remembered. But when a whisper crawls out from inside a wall... forgetting stops being an option.

It happened two days after the library.

School had ended, and most students were already rushing home. I had just closed my locker when I heard it—soft, raspy, and closer than before.

This time, I didn't run.

Instead, I stood still. I held my breath. And I listened.

"Help..."

I froze.

The voice wasn't coming from behind me or around the corner. It was coming from inside the wall. Right between my locker and the one next to it.

Then it came again. This time slower. More broken.

"Please... help me..."

I stepped back, heart hammering. But not from fear—at least not entirely. This time, I wanted to know.

I didn't want to face it alone, though.

I pulled out my phone and messaged James.

me: come to the lockers. now.
james: bro why
me: bring will, john and mike. just come.

Five minutes later, they showed up, backpacks slung lazily over their shoulders. James was eating chips.

"You look like you saw a ghost," he said with a grin, crunching loudly.

"I heard something," I said, voice low. "Again."

Will raised an eyebrow. "Another whisper?"

"Yeah. Right here. Just now. From inside the wall."

James stopped chewing.

"You're serious?"

"I wouldn't call you all the way here for fun."

We stood there in silence for a moment.

Mike looked at the locker. "Maybe it's pipes."

"No pipes whisper help me," I said sharply.

John shifted on his feet. "You sure it wasn't your imagination? You've been kind of... tense lately."

"I know what I heard."

Then it came again.

So faint it was almost nothing.

"Please..."

We all heard it.

James dropped his chip bag.

"Nope. Nope. Nope."

But instead of running, he stayed.

I looked at them all. "We need to follow it."

"What do you mean follow it?" Mike asked, his voice tight. "It's a wall. We can't just walk through it."

"No," I said. "But it's leading somewhere. Last time I heard it, it was near the lockers. Now it's in the wall. If we walk along the hall, maybe we'll hear it again."

The others looked uneasy, but they followed as I began walking. We moved slowly, pressing our ears to the wall every few steps like idiots. A teacher passed by and gave us a weird look but didn't say anything.

Then James stopped cold.

"Guys," he whispered. "Listen."

We pressed in.

It was clearer now. Not just whispers. Words.

"Down... it's cold... help..."

The voice was moving. Or leading. Deeper into the school.

We followed.

Through the long corridor behind the science labs. Past the janitor's closet. Toward the gym.

The closer we got, the colder the air felt. Not the usual kind of cold—this was damp, like the chill of a basement or a crawl space that hadn't seen light in years.

When we reached the gym doors, the voice stopped.

All four of us stood there, breathing heavy. The hallway was dead silent.

"Why the gym?" Will asked, looking pale.

"I don't know," I said. "But we're here now."

Mike hesitated. "It's probably nothing. Just old building noises messing with us."

"Then why does it keep saying 'help me'?" I asked.

He didn't answer.

James pushed open the double doors to the gym. The metal creaked like a warning. Inside, the gym was dark—just faint daylight filtering in through the high windows. Our footsteps echoed across the polished floor as we stepped inside.

Nothing looked strange. The bleachers were pushed back. The basketball hoops hung still. There was no one else there.

But it felt wrong.

"I don't like this," John whispered. "It feels like we're being watched."

We moved to the center of the gym, huddled together like kids on a dare. The silence felt too heavy. Too sharp around the edges.

Then James whispered, “Over there.”

He pointed to a square outline near the far wall—a trap door, maybe, or a maintenance hatch. Almost invisible from far away. None of us had noticed it before.

We walked over slowly.

It was a metal plate, flush with the wooden floor. No label. No handle. Just a faint seam around the edges and four heavy bolts.

“I didn’t know this was here,” I said.

“Neither did I,” said James. “And I’ve been here since sixth grade.”

I knelt beside it and brushed away the dust.

That’s when we heard the sound again.

Not a whisper.

Knocking.

Three slow knocks. From beneath the floor.

John jumped back, eyes wide. "Okay. That's it. We're leaving. This is insane."

"No," I said. "We're not done."

"Bro, there's something under the gym," Mike said, voice shaking. "That's not normal."

"I know. That's why we can't stop now."

Another knock.

Then silence.

We all stood there, barely breathing.

"What's under here?" James finally asked. "Storage?"

"Basement," I said. "I think this is how they sealed it."

They looked at me.

“I talked to someone,” I continued. “At the library. She used to go to this school. She said there used to be a pool in the basement. But they closed it off. Welded the doors. Said a kid went missing down there.”

“Dude,” James said. “That’s not funny.”

“I’m not joking.”

A long pause. Then he said, “So... what now?”

I looked back at the trapdoor.

“I’m going to find a way in.”

Nobody spoke.

Then James sighed. “I hate this. I really hate this. But I’m not letting you go alone.”

John groaned. “This is how people die in movies.”

But one by one, they all nodded.

Even scared, they stayed.

And somewhere beneath our feet, in the dark, something waited.

05

Chapter

✦

The Drawer

Knock.

Knock.

Knock.

The sound echoed beneath the gym floor like a heartbeat—slow, steady, real.

We stood frozen for a moment. None of us spoke. Even James, who always had something to say, looked pale.

Will was the first to whisper, "Guys... we need to get out of here."

But I stepped forward instead, eyes locked on the square metal outline we had found in the floor—the hatch, or whatever it was. I knelt beside it, dragging my fingers along the seam.

"No handle. It's sealed from the top," I muttered.

"Good," Will said. "That means it's supposed to stay closed."

James glanced around. "There's gotta be a way in. If they sealed this, maybe there's another way... a side entrance? Or a utility room?"

That's when I remembered something.

"The storage room," I said suddenly. "The one beside the gym. I saw it once after PE, when the janitor left the door open. It goes deeper than it looks. Maybe even underneath."

Mike's eyebrows lifted. "And you think it leads down to... the pool?"

"Maybe. But we won't know unless we check."

James nodded, already walking. "Let's go."

Will groaned behind us. "Why do I feel like we're walking straight into a horror movie?"

The hallway outside the gym was quiet. Too quiet. We moved fast, trying not to make noise, ducking past the rows of lockers and heading toward the rusted door labeled Equipment Storage - Authorized Personnel Only.

I reached for the handle.

Locked.

Of course.

I rattled it anyway, just in case. No luck.

"Guess that's that," Will said, already turning away.

But Mike stepped forward. "Hold up."

He unzipped his backpack and pulled out a pencil case. From inside, he took two paperclips and straightened them quickly, his hands surprisingly steady.

“I saw a tutorial once,” he said, kneeling beside the padlock. “Guy picked a whole set of locks with these things. I’ve been wanting to try it.”

Will gawked. “You what? You’re learning to break into places?”

“Better than standing here doing nothing,” Mike muttered, pushing one clip into the lock and twisting the other inside with a few delicate tugs.

Click.

We all leaned in.

Click.

James whistled low under his breath. “If you open this, I’m buying you lunch for a week.”

Mike didn't answer. His brow was furrowed. He shifted the clips again.

Click.

The lock popped open with a soft clunk.

Mike grinned. "You owe me tacos."

"Deal," James said.

Will stared, mouth slightly open. "We're all going to jail."

I pulled the padlock off and pushed the door open slowly.

A musty, metallic smell drifted out. The kind that clings to forgotten places. Inside, it was dark—barely lit by a single buzzing bulb overhead. Old wrestling mats leaned against the walls. Tall racks were filled with tangled nets, ball carts, and old PE equipment draped in dust.

The door creaked closed behind us with a soft click. I didn't like that sound.

We moved together, pushing deeper into the room.

"This place gives me the creeps," John muttered. "Why is it so big?"

"Storage," James said, shining his phone flashlight ahead. "For creepy secrets, apparently."

Then we saw it—at the very back of the room.

A metal filing cabinet, tall and gray and dented like it had been kicked a few times. A faded label on the top drawer read:

ADMIN - ARCHIVE

I stepped forward, heart racing, and grabbed the top handle. It groaned loudly as I pulled.

Inside: a mess of papers, old folders, laminated schedules, and dusty attendance records.

"Help me look," I said.

We rifled through them quickly, flipping open envelopes, skimming pages.

"Nothing useful," James muttered, tossing aside a folder labeled Track and Field Budgets, 1997.

Then, from the second drawer down, I spotted a worn newspaper clipping tucked between some loose sheets.

I pulled it out carefully.

The headline was faded but still legible:
"Westbridge Student Disappears. Ongoing Investigation."

There was a photo. Blurry. Grainy. A boy, probably around our age. Hoodie. Dark eyes. Standing near a row of lockers.

My chest tightened.

The article was short. Barely a paragraph. It didn't say how he disappeared. No date. Just a name: Evan R.
Last seen near the gym. No confirmed sightings since.

I stared at it, then passed it around.

James read it and handed it off quickly, face unreadable. "This is... it?"

Will scanned it, frowning. "That's all? One paragraph?"

Mike held it last, shaking his head. "No police report? No follow-up? Just... that?"

"This isn't nothing," I said. "This proves he was real."

James rubbed the back of his neck. "I was expecting something else. Something bigger. Secret tunnels. Blueprints. Not one dusty article."

"We heard the knocking," I snapped. "We know something's down there."

"And now we know someone was down there," Mike said. "But there's no proof he died. Or even that it was connected to the pool."

Will folded his arms. "So what do we do now? Break through the gym floor? Dig a tunnel? I'm out, man. This isn't fun anymore."

The air felt heavier now. Like reality was closing back in.

"Let's just go," John muttered. "It's getting late."

No one argued.

We quietly pushed the drawer shut and slipped out of the storage room. I locked it behind us and slid the padlock back into place.

By the time we left the school, the sun had started to set, casting long shadows across the empty field. No one talked much as we walked our separate ways.

When I got home, I sat on my bed and unfolded the article again. I ran my thumb across Evan's name.

No one believed there was more to the story.

But I knew there was.

Somewhere beneath that gym... Evan was still waiting.

06

Chapter

✦

The Hollow Ones

The library was almost empty when I arrived after school.

A cold drizzle slicked the pavement outside, and the clouds rolled low and gray, muffling the light. I shook off my hoodie and stepped into the silence. That same heavy, watchful quiet pressed in around me like it always did here.

I didn't go to the shelves this time. I went straight to the same table in the back, beneath the flickering bulb, where the Local History section stood guard with its dusty secrets.

I pulled the same thick book from the shelf—The History of Westbridge—and opened to the familiar spot. Pages 136 and 137. Still broken. Still wrong.

So I started looking for something else. Anything else.

I scoured the indexes of other books. Checked the town census records. Even the ancient town planning logs.

Minutes blurred into hours. My eyes ached from reading. The sound of the rain against the windows faded into the background like white noise.

That's when I felt her presence again.

"Still digging?" the library lady asked gently.

I jumped slightly. She was standing beside me, holding a small mug of tea, her cardigan draped loosely over her shoulders. Her voice was calm, but something about the way she looked at me told me she already knew what I was searching for.

"I have to know," I said. "About Evan. About the pool. About the knocking."

She nodded slowly. "Most kids get scared and stop. But you're not most kids, are you?"

I didn't answer. I couldn't.

She glanced around the empty room, then leaned closer. "There's a room here. One no one uses anymore. Wasn't always part of the library—it used to be a record room for state workers. Historical preservation division, they called it. But they were really just data cleaners."

"Data cleaners?" I asked.

"People hired to erase things," she said simply. "To rewrite the past. Change names. Seal files. Burn others."

My mouth felt dry. "Why are you telling me this?"

She looked me in the eye. "Because I went to that school. And because I think you're ready."

Then, from her sweater pocket, she pulled out a small brass key attached to a faded leather tag.

Room B12.

"It's in the basement," she said. "Go quietly. And don't stay too long."

I took the key, hands shaking slightly. "Thank you."

She smiled faintly, but there was no warmth in it. Just tiredness. "Some doors, once opened, never quite close again."

The basement hallway beneath the library felt older than the rest of the building. The walls were thicker. The air was colder. I followed the narrow passage until I found the door—Room B12—its paint chipped, the number almost worn away.

I unlocked it with a soft click and pushed it open.

Inside was a small, windowless room filled with metal cabinets, binders, and boxes labeled with dates going back decades. A single light bulb hung from the ceiling, swinging slightly as if someone had just left.

I scanned the shelves and found a file marked Westbridge Middle - Classified Internal Reports.

Inside: a stack of photocopied documents. Dozens of pages. Faint stamps marked with REDACTED, INTERNAL ONLY, and DO NOT DUPLICATE.

I sat at the dusty desk and began to read.

Annual Incident Review - Westbridge Middle School - Internal Use Only

Year: 2005

Total Missing Persons: 6

Ages: 11-13

Incident Type: Unexplained Disappearances

Public Cover Story: Gas leak - evacuation - temporary student transfers.

Official Investigation: None

Final Status: CASE CLOSED

Year: 2006

Total Missing Persons: 6

Cover Story: Bus rerouting - family relocation notices issued retroactively.

Final Status: CASE CLOSED

Every year. Six students.

Different cover-ups. Different lies. But always the same number.

Then I saw it.

Subject: Group Formation - "The Hollow Ones"

My heart skipped a beat.

The Hollow Ones are believed to be a student-initiated group formed sometime in the late 1990s. Membership is limited to six individuals. Purpose unknown. Believed to involve unsanctioned after-hours activity centered in the disused pool facility. Initial leader identified as EVAN R. (Full name redacted).

Eyewitness accounts from former janitor (name withheld) report ritualistic dares performed at night, often involving isolation, water submersion, and underground access points. At least three known members went missing during the academic year. Others allegedly disappeared during summer break.

Cover narrative maintained by local authorities in cooperation with internal school board. No external press coverage permitted. Families compensated. Witnesses silenced.

I swallowed hard, my hands trembling as I turned the page.

There were diagrams. Sketches of the pool layout. Security footage logs—most of them blacked out or labeled "Unrecoverable."

One hand-written note caught my eye.

"The Hollow Ones never disbanded. If the leader remains, so does the door. So does the hunger."

I sat there, stunned.

They weren't just ghost stories.

They weren't whispers in the dark.

They were real. And someone—Evan—had started it.

But why?

I didn't know yet.

But I did know this: someone had been covering it all up for years. The school. The police. Maybe even people higher up. They created distractions, fake news, empty explanations to hide the truth.

And kids kept disappearing.

I stood, heart pounding.

I wasn't just afraid anymore. I was angry.

No one else knew what I now knew. And if no one stopped Evan—if he was still there—then six more names could vanish by the end of the year.

I couldn't let that happen.

I had a new goal now.

Find Evan. Uncover the truth. And end this.

07

Chapter

✦

You're Next

It started like any other day.

The sky was unusually blue, the sun too bright for how I felt inside. Students trickled into the halls, laughing, shouting, brushing past each other with backpacks slung over one shoulder. Teachers stood by classroom doors, sipping coffee, nodding hello.

But nothing felt normal to me anymore.

Not after what I read in Room B12.

Not after learning the truth about The Hollow Ones.

I walked through the halls like a ghost, eyes scanning every shadow, every vent, every darkened corner. Evan's name echoed in my mind like a warning bell.

No one else knew. But I knew.

And that made me a target.

I was heading to third period when I ducked into the bathroom—mostly to clear my head. The fluorescent lights above buzzed overhead, flickering slightly. The place was empty. Just me and the echo of my own footsteps on tile.

I turned on the faucet, splashed cold water on my face, and looked up at the mirror.

Then I froze.

There, in the condensation on the glass, just above the sink—someone had scratched something into the mirror.

At first it looked like random lines. But then I stepped closer.

YOU'RE NEXT.

The letters were jagged. Uneven. Like they'd been carved with a key or the edge of a coin.

My mouth went dry. I stepped back, heart pounding.

This wasn't a prank.

No one else knew what I knew.

Which meant someone had been watching me.

Someone... like Evan.

I turned, scanning the room—nothing. The stalls were empty. The room was silent, save for the soft drip-drip-drip of a leaking sink in the corner.

Then, faintly, I heard it again.

A whisper.

Not words. Just a sound. Breath against the wall.

Like something exhaling through cracked tile.

I grabbed my bag and bolted out the door.

—

By lunch, I had pulled the others into the far corner of the cafeteria. The noise of the other students seemed miles away.

"I saw it," I said. "On the mirror. Someone scratched it in."

"Wait, what?" James asked, mouth still full of pizza.

"You're next. That's what it said. In the mirror. Someone knows I found the files. They're warning me."

Will immediately looked panicked. "Okay, that's it. You need to stop. We need to stop. This is going way too far."

“No,” I said sharply. “This proves it. We’re not crazy. Evan is real. The Hollow Ones are real. And they know I’ve seen the truth.”

Mike leaned in, lowering his voice. “So... what now?”

I looked at them, each one of them. I could see the fear in their eyes—but I could also see the same thing I felt: determination.

“We do the ritual,” I said.

James blinked. “Wait—you’re serious?”

“I found a partial description of it in the file. It said the Hollow Ones performed the ritual at night. In the pool.”

“And how are we even supposed to get into a pool that doesn’t exist?” Will asked, his voice cracking slightly.

“We break in. Through the gym. Maybe through that hatch. Maybe there’s another entrance.”

Mike nodded slowly. “If Evan started this, maybe we can end it the same way it began."

Will buried his face in his hands. "This is insane."

"Maybe," I said. "But I'd rather be insane than next."

The bell rang.

As we grabbed our trays and backpacks, I turned to the others and said the words I wasn't sure I'd ever say:

"Meet me at the school tonight. Midnight. Bring flashlights. And whatever you need to be brave."

James tried to smile. "Do jokes count?"

"No," I said. "Not tonight."

That night, as I packed my flashlight, extra batteries, gloves, and the news article about Evan, my hands shook—not from fear, but from anticipation.

Something had begun, and now there was no turning back.

By morning, everything would be different.

One way or another.

08

Chapter

✦

The Pool

The school was darker than I'd ever seen it.

At midnight, the hallways were no longer just hallways—they were tunnels of shadow, lined with lockers that looked like silent sentinels. Our flashlights cut thin beams through the dark as we moved together, step by step.

"Why does it feel like the school is watching us?" Will whispered, glancing around.

"Because it probably is," James said with a nervous laugh,

though his voice cracked halfway through. “Don’t worry. If a ghost shows up, I’ll... uh, tell it a joke.”

“Ghosts don’t laugh,” Mike muttered, pushing the gym doors open.

John was the last one in. He paused at the threshold, shining his light across the vast, empty gym. “This is a bad idea,” he said softly. “I know I agreed... but this feels wrong.”

“You can still leave,” I told him.

He looked at me, then at the others. “I’m not letting you all go in alone. But if something jumps out, I will scream.”

The gym was silent, the wooden floor gleaming faintly under the flashlight beams. We all stopped near the center, where the faint square outline of the hatch was barely visible.

“There it is,” I said, pointing.

“Yeah, and it’s still locked,” Will said. “We can’t just—”

Before he finished, Mike crouched, pulling two paper clips from his pocket with a grin. "You really think I came unprepared? I watched two more lockpicking videos this time."

James smirked. "Great. If we die tonight, at least we'll know who to blame."

"Remind me again why we trust him with locks?" John said, raising an eyebrow.

"Because," Mike said, working on the bolts, "I'm the only one here with paper clips and YouTube Premium."

Click.

Another bolt gave way.

We all leaned in, silent. The tension in the air was thicker than the darkness around us.

Then—click. CLANK.

The final bolt snapped open.

The hatch groaned.

A gust of air escaped—cool, damp, and smelling faintly of chlorine and rust.

"Holy..." James whispered. "This is real."

Will took a step back. "Guys. No. This is where people die in horror movies."

"I'm not turning around now," I said. "If Evan's down there, this is our chance."

Mike adjusted his backpack straps. "You're not going alone."

I looked at them all—James, Mike, Will, John.

John exhaled slowly. "This is going to haunt us forever, isn't it?"

"Let's find out," I said.

We descended.

The staircase was steep and narrow, walls close on either side, cold to the touch. Each step echoed, metal against our shoes. The air grew colder as we went, thicker with moisture. When we reached the bottom, a metal door stood ahead, cracked open.

James pushed it with two fingers. “If this slams shut behind us, I’m suing a ghost.”

I held my breath and stepped in.

And there it was.

A pool.

Still. Clean. Lit by soft, flickering ceiling lights that shouldn’t have worked after all these years. The water glowed faintly. It was beautiful, in the most unnerving way possible.

“This... this should be disgusting,” Mike said. “Like, filled with sludge and rats.”

“Yeah,” John muttered. “Instead it looks like a spa from hell.”

Will just stared at it, pale. “I don’t like this. This isn’t natural.”

“No,” I said. “But it’s real.”

We gathered at the edge. The floor tiles were icy under our feet. I pulled out the handwritten ritual notes from my jacket pocket and unfolded them with trembling fingers.

“We form a circle,” I said. “Hold hands. Recite the words.”

“Seriously?” John said, eyebrows raised. “We’re really doing this?”

“Yes.”

Mike nodded. “Let’s get it over with.”

James sighed. “Look, if a water demon eats me, someone better tell my mom I died trying to solve a supernatural mystery.”

One by one, we stepped into the water. The chill hit like electricity—clean, sharp, immediate. We waded until it reached our waists. Our breaths came out in little clouds.

We joined hands. The circle closed.

“You guys good?” I asked.

Will looked like he wanted to cry. “Define ‘good.’”

“I’m here,” John said quietly. “Let’s finish this.”

We all closed our eyes.

I took a breath and began.

“We call to the one who lingers.”

The others repeated.

“We call to the one who sees.”

Again.

“We call to the one who waits.”

Our voices echoed across the tiled walls.

Then silence.

The water stilled. The air felt heavy. We stood perfectly still, shivering in place, waiting for something—anything.

"Now what?" James asked.

"I don't kno—"

That's when the water stirred.

Not from us.

Something beneath us shifted.

"Did you feel that?" Will whispered, his grip like iron.

"Yes," John breathed. "It wasn't us."

Then we heard it.

A voice.

Faint. From the deep.

"...Why did you call me?"

We all froze.

"Guys." James said in a shaking voice. "That... wasn't one of us."

"Don't break the circle," I said, my voice firm now. "Whatever happens—stay together."

And below the surface, something began to rise.

09

Chapter

✦

The Rope

The door opened with a sigh, like the world itself exhaling.

Behind it wasn't darkness—not exactly. It was something thinner than reality, like a dream barely stitched together. We stepped through, side by side, the five of us.

The space inside was gray and shifting. The floor wasn't solid—it moved like mist beneath our feet, but we didn't fall. Shapes flickered in and out of existence. Walls formed, then melted. Desks. Hallways. Streetlamps. All dissolving like breath on glass.

“It’s not real,” Mike whispered.

“No,” I said. “It’s memory.”

There, suspended in the air before us like a forgotten thread, was a rope.

Thick. Frayed. Hanging in midair and stretching out into the fog, trailing endlessly forward.

We followed it.

Each step brought the memory into focus.

We saw a boy sitting alone at lunch—head down, tray untouched. Evan.

We saw him at recess, sitting under the old oak tree. A group of kids laughed nearby, not unkindly—but they never looked at him. Like he didn’t exist.

“I never noticed him,” Will whispered.

"None of us did," John replied quietly.

More steps. More memory.

A kitchen—quiet, warm. His mother smiling.

Then a hospital room. Machines beeping.

His father, fading.

Another step.

An empty hallway. Evan holding a framed photo to his chest, sitting on the floor outside a locked door, shaking silently.

James murmured, "He lost everything."

More rope.

It led us deeper, through flickering fragments of Evan's life—his silence, his loneliness, the way the world ignored him until he vanished into it.

And then we saw the figure.

Standing at the very end of the rope.

Evan.

He looked just like we remembered from the news clipping. Hoodie. Shadowed eyes. But here, he was whole. Not a ghost. Not a monster.

Just a boy.

He didn't move. Just stared at us.

And then he whispered.

So soft, it barely reached us.

"They only saw me when I disappeared."

The rope curled at his feet like a noose.

He looked down, then up at us—his expression not angry, but

empty.

"I just wanted to belong."

And then, he was gone.

Vanished like smoke.

A single click echoed behind us.

We turned.

A door had appeared in the wall of memory—simple, white, glowing faintly.

I looked at my friends.

None of us said a word.

We stepped through together.

Light.

Cold air.

And then—

Beep-beep-beep-beep.

My alarm.

My eyes snapped open.

Sunlight poured through my bedroom window. The clock blinked: 7:00 AM.

My heart pounded.

My sheets were tangled. My clothes still damp from the pool water.

I sat up, breath caught between two worlds.

Was it a dream?

Or had we crossed into something real... and come back

changed?

I didn't know yet.

But I would find out.

10

Chapter

✦

The Morning After

The sunlight felt warmer than it had in weeks.

I sat on the front steps of my house, a cup of juice in my hands, just watching the world. Birds chirped. A dog barked down the street. Sprinklers ticked lazily across someone's lawn.

Everything looked normal.

But I wasn't sure if I was.

School came and went like it always did. Lockers slamming.

Teachers talking. Friends laughing. Nothing had changed.

Except it had.

James nudged me during math class. "So... uh, did we dream that?"

"I don't know," I said.

Mike leaned over from the other side. "My shoes were still wet this morning."

"I still have the marker I used to draw in that memory," Will added at lunch. "It's in my pocket."

John said nothing, but he gave me a look across the table. One that said, We all remember. We were there.

We didn't talk about it much after that.

We didn't have to.

That weekend, I went back to the gym alone.

Just to see.

The floor was solid. Seamless. No sign of the hatch.

Like it had never existed.

I stood at center court for a while, listening. But there was no whisper. No knocking.

Just the distant hum of the old lights overhead.

Maybe Evan had let go.

Maybe we had helped him.

Or maybe the door had simply closed—for now.

That night, I took Caramel's old photo from the drawer and placed it on my nightstand. I didn't cry. I just looked at it, thinking how things sometimes leave us, but never really go.

Memories stay.

And sometimes, so do we.

One week later, James texted the group chat:

james: if any of u say “we should go back” I’m blocking u

mike: chill. we saved reality. we’re retired now

will: just don’t bring a knife to class again lol

john: i still think about the rope

me: I still see the door sometimes.
in dreams.
but I don’t open it.

No one replied for a while.

Then James sent a final message:

good.

And that was enough.

제 1장

✦

세상은 내 편이 아니야

세상은 내 편이 아니다.

우리 가족은 아빠의 직장 때문에 이사를 결정했다. 아무런 경고도, 변명의 기회도 없이. 그냥 골판지 상자와 마감일뿐이었다. 새로운 시작을 향한 한 걸음 한 걸음은 무거운 사슬을 끄는 듯한 느낌이었다—사슬의 고리는 모든 친구, 모든 안에만 통하는 농담, 어두운 가로등 아래 늦은 밤 산책들로 이루어져 있었다.

부모님은 아무 일도 아닌 것처럼 행동했다. "금방 새 친구 사귈 수 있을 거야."라고 했다. 하지만 나는 그저 과거를 지우고 아무 일 없었던 것처럼 새롭게 시작할 수 없었다. 나는 새 출발이 아니라, 내 삶을 되찾고 싶었다.

방 하나하나가 비어 갔다. 우리의 것이었던 물건들이 하나둘 사라졌다. 내 포스터는 없어졌고, 책들은 포장되었으며, 익숙했던 웃음소리는 점점 사라져 갔다.

하지만 무시할 수 없는 공간이 하나 있었다.

거실 한쪽 구석, 창가 근처의 나무 바닥. 색이 바래고 시간이 지나면서 반질반질해진 그 자리는 페인트가 벗겨지고 벽지가 벗겨져 있었으며 방 안 다른 곳보다 더 차가웠다. 하지만 캐러멜에게 그곳은 특별한 자리였다.

나는 학교에서 돌아오면 늘 거기에 누워 햇볕을 쬐고 있는 캐러멜을 보았다. 문 여는 소리에 고개를 들었다가, 다시 꼬리를 흔들고 잠들곤 했다. 가끔은 코를 골고, 가끔은 다리를 꿈틀거리며 무언가를 쫓는 꿈을 꾸는 듯했다. 나는 늘 그가 무슨 꿈을 꾸는지 궁금했다. 풀밭을 달리는 꿈? 누군가를 쫓는 꿈? 아니면 그냥 햇빛 속에 따뜻하게 누워 있는 꿈?

그는 항상 내 마음속에 남아 있을 것이다.

이사 당일, 나는 차 뒷좌석에 앉아 창밖만 바라보며 아무 말도 하지 않았다. 익숙했던 이웃을 지날 때마다 가슴이 조여 왔다. 모퉁이의 작은 가게, 삐걱거리는 그네가 있는 놀이터, 그리고 캐러멜을 처음 데려왔던 애완동물 가게의 삐뚤어진 간판까지.

나는 울지 않았다. 하지만 마음속은 무거웠다.

공항에 도착했을 때, 나는 고개를 숙이고 부모님의 가짜 미소도 보지 않으려 했다. 낯선 사람들 앞에서 울고 싶지 않았기에, 모든 감정을 닫아 버렸다. 마치 누군가의 꿈속으로 걸어 들어가는 것처럼 비행기에 몸을 실었다.

새로운 곳은... 그럭저럭 괜찮았다. 작은 학교, 조용한 거리, 그리고 근처에 큰 호수가 있었다. 아빠와 나는 주말마다 낚시를 하러 갔다. 나는 별로 말이 없었지만, 아빠는 함께 있는 걸 좋아하시는 것 같았다.

그러다 제임스를 만났다.

그 애는 좀 이상한 애였다. 항상 농담을 하고, 이상한 이야기를 지어냈다. 언젠가는 호수에서 자동차만 한 물고기를 봤다고 했는데, 이내 웃으며 "아니면 그냥 통나무였을지도? 근데 아주 수상한 통나무였어."라고 덧붙였다. 가끔은 웃음이 사라지고 아주 진지한 표정을 지을 때도 있었다. 하지만 대부분은... 그냥 함께 있기에 괜찮은 친구였다.

어느 날, 그는 나에게 방과 후 자기 집에 오라고 했다. 우리는 가방을 내려놓고 옛날 공포 게임을 함께 했다—예상 가능한 점프 스케어가 있어도 여전히 놀라는 그런 게임이었다.

어느 장면에서 깜짝 놀란 뒤, 제임스는 장난기 어린 미소를 지으며 말했다.

“너 이 학교 저주받았다는 얘기 들어 봤어?”

나는 눈썹을 치켜올렸다. “뭐라고?”

그는 고개를 끄덕였다. “진짜야. 한 10년쯤 전에 학생 하나가 사라졌대. 휙—그냥 사라졌어. 아무도 못 찾았대. 어떤 사람들은 아직도 학교 안에 있다고 해.”

나는 눈을 굴렸다. “설마 유령이 돼서 떠돈다는 얘기야?”

제임스는 잠시 나를 바라보다가 어깨를 으쓱했다. “아마도? 잘 몰라. 근데 이상한 소리 들었다는 사람도 있어. 벽에서 소리 나고, 속삭임 들리고, 긁는 소리도 나고… 곧 알게 될 거야.”

나는 웃어넘겼다.

그냥 장난치는 줄 알았다.

하지만 지금은… 잘 모르겠다.

제 2장

✦

첫 번째 징조

그건 싸움으로 시작됐다.

그럴 의도는 없었다. 솔직히 말하면, 나는 문제를 일으키는 성격이 아니다. 하지만 누군가가 네 가족에 대해—그것도 아무것도 모르면서—헛소리를 하면, 사람은 항상 이성적으로 판단할 수 없다.

그 애 이름은 데릭이었다. 자기가 생각하는 것보다 훨씬 유쾌하지도 않으면서 계속 말장난을 하고, 사람들의 신경을 긁는 걸 즐기는 그런 타입. 우리 아빠에 대해 멍청한 농담을 했다. 우리가 이사 온 게 “돈이 다 떨어졌기 때문”이라나. 나는 넘기려 했다. 진심으로 참아 보려 했다.

그런데 그는 캐러멜에 대해 말하기 시작했다. 걔가 어떻게 알았는지도 모르겠다. 아마 제임스가 언급했을 수도 있고, 내가 한 말일 수도 있다. 하지만 그는 이렇게 말했다.

"그 잡종은 진작에 두고 와야 했지. 개도 포기할 땐 안다고."

피가 거꾸로 솟았다.

정신을 차려 보니, 나는 그 위에 올라타 있었고, 주먹은 불끈 쥐고 있었으며, 무슨 말을 외치고 있었지만 기억도 나지 않았다. 선생님이 날 떼어 냈다. 데릭은 피 묻은 입술과 함께, 마치 자기가 바라던 대로 흘러간 것처럼 만족스러운 미소를 지었다.

나는 방과 후 벌을 받았다.

방과 후의 학교는 달랐다.

훈계. 그리고 숙제를 마칠 때까지 홀로 남아야 한다는 벌칙.

평소의 분주한 발소리, 락커 문 닫히는 소리, 수백 명의 수다가 사라졌다. 그 고요함은 평온함이 아니라 공허함이었다. 마치 건물 전체가 숨을 죽인 듯했다. 천장 조명은 희미하게 윙윙거렸고, 몇 번 깜빡였다. 교실 문이 줄지어 있는 복도를 지날 때마다 모든 소리가 과장되어 들렸다. 내 발걸음. 바닥이 삐걱거리는 소리. 심지어 가방 지퍼 여는 소리마저 너무 컸다.

나는 내 락커에 가서 워크북을 꺼내려 했다.

그때 그걸 보았다.

깊고, 흉측하고, 선명했다.

마치 누군가가 칼을 박고 쭉 그어 내린 것처럼, 락커 안쪽 벽에 새겨져 있었다. 나무는 속살이 드러나고, 갈라져 있었다. 나는 멍하니 그것을 바라보았다. 전에 본 적은 없었다. 그런 건 분명 눈에 띄었을 것이다.

그리고 그때,

나는 그 소리를 들었다.

속삭임.

크지 않았다. 명확하지도 않았다. 하지만 분명 있었다. 숨을 내쉬는 듯한, 흐릿한, 뭔가가 락커 뒤... 혹은 벽 안에서 들려오는 듯한 소리.

나는 얼어붙었다.

머릿속은 '바람이겠지'라고 말했다. '환풍기가 켜졌나 보다'라고도.

하지만 직감은 달랐다. 바람이 아니었다. 기계음도 아니었다.

그건,

목소리였다.

나는 뒤를 홱 돌아보았다.

아무도 없었다. 복도는 텅 비어 있었다.

나는 락커에서 물러났다. 심장은 북처럼 뛰고 있었다.

나는 책을 낚아채듯 꺼내 들고 락커 문을 쾅 닫았다. 그 소리는 총소리처럼 복도에 울려 퍼졌다.

기다리지 않았다. 빠르게 걸었다. 거의 뛰다시피 했다.

그날 밤, 나는 제임스에게 메시지를 보냈다.

나 학교에 뭔가 있어

제임스 오 노 ㅋㅋ 유령 찾았네

나 진지해. 내 락커에 긁힌 자국 있었어. 속삭임도 들었고. 장난 아냐

제임스 뭐라고 속삭였는데?

나 못 알아들었어. 근데 진짜였어

제임스 실종된 애가 네 수학 노트 빌리려던 거 아냐? ㅋㅋ

당연히 농담이었다.

하지만 나는 웃을 수 없었다.

다음 날 점심시간, 나는 존, 윌, 마이크에게 이야기했다.

그들은 예의상 들어 줬다. 하지만 눈을 피하며 서로를 슬쩍 바라보는 눈빛이 모든 걸 말해 줬다.

윌 : 그냥 오래된 환풍기 소리일걸.

존 : 그래. 아니면 누가 장난친 거겠지. 데릭 친구들이라든가.

마이크 : 힘든 한 주 보냈잖아. 뇌가 장난친 걸 수도 있어.

나는 반박하지 않았다.

그날 오후, 나는 락커를 다시 열어 봤다.

긁힌 자국은 여전히 있었다.
하지만 이번엔 다른 게 보였다.

희미한 얼룩—손자국처럼 보였다.
그런데 손가락이 너무 길었다. 마치 뼈가 없는 것처럼.
무언가가 금속 표면을 스르르 기어간 듯 번져 있었다.

그날 밤, 쉽게 잠들 수 없었다.

나는 침대에 누워 천장을 바라보았다.
방구석의 그림자들은 평소보다 더 어두워 보였다.
스탠드를 켜 놓은 채 잠을 청했다. 단지 편안함 때문이라 생각했지만,

실은 스위치를 끄는 게 두려웠다.

창문은 닫혀 있었지만, 벽 너머 어딘가에서 속삭임 같은 희미한 소리가 들리는 것만 같았다.

그럴 리 없었다.

나는 스스로에게 스트레스 때문이라고 말했다.
싸움 때문에 아드레날린이 남아서 그렇다고.
하지만 눈을 감을 때마다 그 긁힌 자국이 떠올랐고, 그 속삭임이 들려왔고, 복도에서 내 뒤에 느꼈던 차가운 기운이 다시 느껴졌다.

나는 몸을 옆으로 돌려, 이불을 꽁꽁 싸맸다. 어릴 때처럼.

그때
나는 캐러멜을 떠올렸다.

그는 매일 밤 내 침대 옆 바닥에 자곤 했다.
그의 고른 숨소리는 항상 나를 편안하게 만들었다.

하지만 이제 그 자리는 비어 있었다.
차가웠다.
그리고 이제 나는 혼자가 아니라고 느꼈다—

그렇다고 해서 위안이 되는 건 아니었다.

마치

무언가가 나를 지켜보고 있는 것 같았다.

기다리고 있는 것처럼.

그리고 스탠드를 켜 둔 채였음에도,

어둠은 어떻게든 틈을 비집고 스며들었다.

제 3장

✦

도서관

나는 잊으려 했다.

속삭임, 락커에 난 긁힌 자국, 그 손자국—분명 내 것이 아닌. 이 모든 게 단지 이사로 인한 스트레스 때문이라고 스스로에게 말했다. 싸움. 외로움. 빈틈을 채우기 위해 뇌가 만들어낸 환상일 뿐이라고.

그리고 한동안은 정말로 그렇게 믿었다.

나는 다시 수업에 들어갔다. 강의를 들었다. 제임스가 늘 하던 이상한 농담을 하면 웃어 보였다. 아무 일도 없는 척 행동했다.

물론, 실제로는 아무렇지 않았지만. 하지만 매일 밤 왜 스탠드를 켜고

자는지 설명하는 것보다, 그냥 괜찮은 척하는 게 더 쉬웠다.

흐린 토요일, 나는 도서관에 있었다.

계획한 것도 아니었다. 사실 평소에도 도서관엔 잘 가지 않았다. 너무 조용하고, 너무 먼지가 많았다. 그리고 항상 시간이 멈춘 듯한 느낌이었다. 마치 수년간 공기조차 움직이지 않은 것처럼. 그런데 그날 아침, 뭔가가 날 밀었다. 목소리도, 설명할 수 있는 감정도 아닌, 그저... 가볍게 등을 떠미는 느낌. 마치 누군가 어깨에 손을 얹고 문 쪽으로 방향을 돌리는 것처럼.

그래서 나는 걸었다.

도서관은 메이플과 3번가 모퉁이에 자리 잡고 있었다. 담쟁이덩굴이 벽을 타고 오르는 오래된 벽돌 건물, 삐걱거리는 녹색 문. 입구 옆에 붙은 청동 명판에는 이렇게 적혀 있었다.

웨스트브리지 공공 도서관 – 1902년 설립

안에 들어서자 오래된 종이와 바닥 왁스 냄새가 코를 찔렀다. 조명은 어두웠고, 내가 발을 디딜 때마다 통로에 메아리처럼 울려 퍼졌다. 나는 데스크에 앉아 있는 여직원에게 고개를 끄덕였지만, 그녀는 십자말풀이에서 눈을 떼지 않았다. 나는 축 처진 책장이 늘어선 사이를 지나 걸었다.

무엇을 찾는지도 몰랐다.

처음엔 과학책을 꺼냈다. 생물학에 관한 책. 다가오는 시험을 위해 공부해 보려 했지만, 단어들이 흐릿하게 뭉개져 아무것도 머릿속에 들어오지 않았다. 생각은 자꾸만 멀어졌다.

그래서 그냥 일어나 걸었다. 계획 없이, 그냥 발길 닿는 대로.

결국 나는 도서관에서도 한 번도 가 보지 않은 구석에 다다랐다. 지역 역사 섹션이었다.

이곳의 책들은 달랐다—더 오래됐고, 더 무거웠으며, 가죽 제본이 갈라져 있었고, 제목은 금박으로 새겨져 있었다. 나는 무심코 손가락으로 책등을 쓸다 보니, 한 권에 눈이 멈췄다.

『웨스트브리지의 역사: 학교, 거리, 그리고 비밀』

마지막 단어에 눈이 멈췄다.
비밀?

나는 그 책을 뽑았다. 두꺼웠다. 수십 년간의 시시한 마을 정보가 담긴 책일지도 모르지만, 나는 그것을 들고 테이블로 돌아갔다. 책을 펼치자, 바스락거리는 소리가 나며 마치 책장이 속삭이는 듯했다.

초반 장들은 마을의 개척자들과 초기 정착민, 오래된 토지 분쟁에 관한 이야기였다. 그리고 이어서 학교에 대한 부분이 나왔다.

그때 나는 그것을 보았다.
웨스트브리지 중학교에 관한 섹션.

나는 몸을 앞으로 숙였다.

책에는 학교가 1956년에 지어졌다고 나와 있었다. 붉은 벽돌로 된 외벽, 넓은 복도, 체육관은 강당 겸용이라는 설명. 그리고 아주 무심하게 이렇게 적혀 있었다.

"1962년, 학교에는 표준 크기의 실내 수영장이 설치되었다..."

잠깐.

무슨 수영장?

나는 미간을 찌푸렸다. 나는 몇 달 동안 웨스트브리지 중학교에 다녔다. 모든 복도를, 모든 문을 다 봤다.
그런 수영장은 없다.

나는 책장을 넘겼다. 135쪽... 136쪽...

그리고 멈췄다.

뭔가 이상했다.

137쪽은 문장 중간에서 시작되었다. 완전히 다른 주제였다. 마치 누군가가 중간을 도려낸 듯했다. 종이는 찢겨 있지 않았지만, 글의 톤이 확 바뀌었고, 시간선도 튀었다. 마치 한 단락—아니, 진실 하나가 빠진 이야기를 읽는 느낌.

나는 다시 앞 페이지로, 그리고 다시 앞으로 넘겼다.

136... 그리고 바로 137.
136쪽 반쪽도 없고, 접힌 자국도 없다. 그냥... 부재.

등골을 타고 차가운 전율이 흘렀다.

나는 도서관 주위를 둘러보았다. 고요했다. 정적이었다.
자연스럽지 않은 고요함. 마치 공간 전체가 또다시 숨을 멈춘 듯한 느낌이었다.

나는 그 부분을 다시 천천히 읽었다.

"1962년에 일련의 사건 이후, 학교에는 표준 크기의 실내 수영장이 설치되었다…"

문장이 거기서 끊겼다.
그다음 줄은 1970년대의 화재 대피 훈련에 관한 내용이었다.
수영장 이야기는 더 이상 없었다.
그 '일련의' 뒤에 이어질 말도 없었다.

무슨 일련의 사건?

사고? 민원? 실종?

그 페이지를 계속 응시할수록, 피부에 소름이 돋았다.

나는 휴대폰으로 검색해 봤다.
하지만 거의 아무것도 나오지 않았다.
피상적인 정보뿐이었다.
수영장에 대한 언급은 없었다.
설계도도, 사진도, 아무것도.

그때 깨달았다—아무도 그 이야기를 하지 않는다는 걸.

학생들도. 선생님들도.
학교 홈페이지에도 없다.

나는 책을 덮고, 생각보다 세게 선반에 꽂아 넣었다.

먼지가 흩날렸다.

공기 속에 뭔가 다시 바뀌었다—차갑고, 미묘하며, 폭풍이 닥치기 직전 같은 날카로움.

내가 도서관을 나서려 할 때, 데스크에 있던 여자가 마침내 고개를 들었다.

그녀의 시선이 내가 왔던 책 섹션을 스쳤다가 다시 나를 바라봤다.

"찾고 있던 거 찾았니?" 그녀가 물었다.

나는 고개를 저었다.

"아직 잘 모르겠어요."

하지만 한 가지는 분명히 알 수 있었다.

웨스트브리지에서 벌어지고 있는 일은 오래전부터 시작된 것이며, 누군가는 그것이 드러나는 걸 원하지 않는다는 것.

내가 도서관을 나서려 돌아섰을 때, 아직도 책 생각이 머릿속을 맴돌고 있었는데—

어떤 목소리가 나를 멈추게 했다.

"무서운 거라도 찾고 있었니?"

나는 눈을 깜빡였다.

십자말풀이에서 고개를 들지 않던 데스크 여직원이 드디어 나를 바라보고 있었다.

안경은 코끝에 내려와 있었고, 은색 머리는 단단히 틀어 올려져 있었다.

그녀의 목소리는 따뜻했지만, 눈빛은 날카로웠다—마치 놓치는 것이 없는 사람처럼.

"그런 것 같아요," 나는 몇 시간 동안의 침묵 탓에 쉰 목소리로 말했다.

그녀는 웃으며 책상 위에서 펜을 두드렸다.

"그 오래된 책에 관심 갖는 애들이 너만 있는 건 아니야. 웨스트브리지의 역사. 제목은 지루하지만, 사람들은 그 안에 마을의 모든 비밀이 숨겨져 있다고 믿더라."

나는 망설였다.

"그 책 읽어 보셨어요?"

그녀는 웃음을 터뜨렸다.

"읽어 봤냐고? 반은 외울 수 있을걸. 나도 웨스트브리지 중학교 나왔어. 오래전 얘기지만."

나는 멈칫했다.

조금 더 다가섰다.

"정말요?"

"으응." 그녀는 의자에 기대며 몸을 살짝 스트레칭했다.

"나는 신관 짓기 전에 졸업했지. 그때는 급식실 의자도 주황색 플라스틱이었는데, 앉을 때마다 삐걱삐걱 소리가 났지."

그녀는 내가 들고 있던 책을 아래로 살펴보고 고개를 약간 기울였다.

"136페이지?" 그녀가 무심한 듯 물었다.

나는 책을 꽉 쥔 손에 힘이 들어갔다.

"네. 그거... 혹시 보셨어요?"

여자는 당장 대답하지 않았다.

그녀의 미소는 조금 사라졌고, 두 손을 단정히 책상 위에 모았다.

"인쇄 오류였다고 하더군," 그녀가 말했다.

"초판 중 몇 부에서 페이지가 하나 누락됐다고."

"그런데 이건 초판이 아니잖아요," 내가 반박했다.

"새로 인쇄된 복사본인데도, 여전히 그 페이지가 빠져 있어요."

그녀는 다시 나를 바라봤다.

이번엔 시선이 더 무겁고, 더 진지했다.

"너, 수영장 얘기 나오는 부분 봤구나?"

나는 천천히 고개를 끄덕였다.

그녀의 목소리가 살짝 낮아졌다.

"대부분 사람들은 그 부분을 그냥 지나쳐. 아니면 대충 읽지. 왜 그런지 알아?"

나는 말하지 않았다.

그저 기다렸다.

"그 수영장은 폐쇄됐거든," 그녀가 말했다.

"개장된 지 얼마 지나지 않아서 말이야. 공식적인 이유는 구조 문제였어—누수, 타일 균열, 배수 문제 같은 것들.

하지만 이 마을에서 자란 사람들은 다 알아.

그게 전부가 아니었다는 걸."

등 뒤로 한기가 스며들었다.

"무슨 일이 있었던 거예요?"

그녀는 망설이다가 천천히 자리에서 일어났다.

무릎에서 작게 뚝 하는 소리가 났고, 그녀는 데스크 뒤를 돌아 나와 내 옆에 섰다.

그녀의 목소리는 낮아졌고, 마치 다른 사람들—아니면 다른 무언가—에게 들리지 않게 하려는 듯 조심스러웠다.

"사건이 하나 있었어," 그녀가 말했다.

"오래전 이야기야. 사람들은 그 얘기를 속삭였지만, 진짜 무슨 일이 있었는지는 아무도 몰랐지.

학교 신문에도 나오지 않았고, 마을 신문에도 안 나왔어.

그런데 내가 중학교 1학년이었을 때였지—조용한 아이 하나가 있었어. 늘 혼자 다녔지.

이름은... 지금은 기억나지 않아."

그녀는 잠시 아래를 바라보았다. 마치 기억을 더듬는 듯이.

"그 애가 사라졌어," 그녀가 계속했다.

"어느 날은 분명히 있었는데, 다음 날은 없어졌지.

도망갔다고 말하는 사람도 있었고, 수영장에서 익사했다고 말하는 사람도 있었어.

하지만 이상한 건... 시신도, 소지품도, 아무것도 발견되지 않았다는 거야. 그냥... 사라졌어."

"수영장에서요?" 나는 속삭이듯 물었다.

그녀는 고개를 끄덕였다.
"사람들은 그렇게 믿었지. 그 애가 수영장에 있었고, 일이 벌어졌을 때 그 안에 있었을 거라고.
우리 중 몇몇은 지금도 그 애가 그 안에 봉인되어 있다고 믿어. 지하층이 봉쇄되었을 때, 함께 갇혔다고."

나는 그녀를 응시했다.
"지하층이요? 우리 학교에는 지하층 없어요."

그녀의 표정이 약간 어두워졌다.

"있어," 그녀가 말했다.
"다만 아무도 그 얘길 하지 않을 뿐이야.
입구는 옛날 유지 관리 구역 근처에 있었어. 청소 도구실을 지나서.
그 철문 뒤에 계단이 있었지.
내가 중2였을 때, 그 문을 용접해서 막았어.
그 이후로는... 마치 처음부터 없었던 것처럼 되었지."

나는 가슴속 공기가 바뀌는 걸 느꼈다. 무언가 무겁게 눌리는 기분.

"그럼 사람들은 왜 기억하지 못하는 거죠?" 내가 물었다.

“왜 인터넷에도 아무것도 없는 거죠?
뉴스도, 졸업 앨범 사진도, 설계도도. 아무것도요.”

그녀는 고개를 저으며 다시 데스크 뒤로 돌아갔다.

“어떤 것들은,” 그녀가 말했다, “묻혀. 일부러 묻히기도 하고.”

나는 그 자리에 멈춰서 그녀를 바라봤다.

“그 애 이름은 기억 안 난다고 하셨죠,” 내가 말했다.
“혹시... 그 밖에 기억나는 게 있나요?”

그녀는 한동안 나를 바라보았다.
그리고 옆 서랍을 열어 오래된 인덱스카드를 하나 꺼냈다.

“도움이 될지 모르겠네,” 그녀가 말했다.
“예전에 학교 관리인이 이야기하는 걸 듣고, 그냥 나 자신에게 남겨 둔 메모야.”

그녀는 그 카드를 내게 건넸다.

거기에는 이렇게 적혀 있었다:

"지하 문은 용접되어 있음.

수영장은 배수되었으나, 락커 하나는 열려 있음.

방은 항상 차가움.

이름은 에릭 또는 에반일 수도 있음.

동쪽 복도는 해 질 무렵 피할 것."

나는 손가락이 약간 떨리는 걸 느끼며, 그 카드를 조심스럽게 접어 주머니에 넣었다.

내가 느끼고 있는 감정이 무엇인지 정확히는 알 수 없었다—두려움일까, 아니면 호기심? 어쩌면 그 둘 다.

하지만 단 한 가지는 확실했다.

그 학교에서 벌어진 일은 단지 '이야기'가 아니었다.

그리고...

그 일은 아직 끝나지 않았다.

제 4장

✦

벽 속의 목소리들

그건 다시 속삭임으로 시작되었다.

크지 않았다. 갑작스럽지도 않았다. 하지만 분명했다.

나는 도서관 직원의 말을 잊으려 애쓰고 있었다. 실종된 소년. 아무도 기억하지 못하는 봉인된 수영장. 하지만 속삭임이 벽 안에서 기어 나올 때... 잊는다는 건 더 이상 선택지가 아니었다.

그 일은 도서관에 간 지 이틀 후에 일어났다.

학교는 끝났고 대부분의 학생들은 집으로 달려가고 있었다. 나는 막 사물함을 닫은 참이었는데—그때 들렸다. 부드럽고, 거칠며, 전보다 더 가까웠다.

이번엔 도망치지 않았다.

대신, 그대로 멈췄다. 숨을 죽였다. 그리고 들었다.

"도와줘..."

몸이 얼어붙었다.

목소리는 내 뒤나 복도 끝에서 오는 게 아니었다. 사물함과 옆 사물함 사이, 바로 그 벽 안에서 들려왔다.

다시 들렸다. 이번엔 더 느리고, 더 깨진 듯한 소리였다.

"제발... 도와줘..."

나는 한 발 뒤로 물러났다. 심장은 두근거렸지만, 이번엔 두려움 때문만은 아니었다.

이번엔, 알고 싶었다.

하지만 혼자 마주하고 싶진 않았다.

나는 핸드폰을 꺼내 제임스에게 메시지를 보냈다.

나 사물함으로 와. 지금.
제임스 야 왜
나 윌, 존, 마이크도 데려와. 그냥 와.

5분 후, 그들은 어깨에 가방을 걸친 채 나타났다. 제임스는 감자칩을 먹고 있었다.

"유령이라도 본 것 같네," 그가 웃으며 말하고, 바삭하게 씹었다.

"뭔가 들었어," 나는 낮게 말했다. "또."

윌이 눈썹을 치켜올렸다. "또 속삭임?"

"응. 바로 여기서. 방금. 벽 안에서."

제임스는 씹던 걸 멈췄다.

"진심이야?"

"장난치려고 너희 다 부른 거 아니야."

우리는 잠시 침묵 속에 서 있었다.

마이크가 사물함을 바라보았다. “배관 소리일 수도 있잖아.”

“‘도와줘’라고 속삭이는 배관은 없어,” 나는 날카롭게 말했다.

존이 발을 옮기며 말했다. “네 상상이었을 수도 있잖아. 요즘 너 좀... 예민하잖아.”

“내가 들은 거 확실해.”

그때, 다시 들렸다.

거의 아무것도 아닌 듯 희미하게.

“제발...”

모두가 들었다.

제임스는 감자칩 봉지를 떨어뜨렸다.

“안 돼. 안 돼. 안 돼.”

하지만 도망치지 않았다.

나는 모두를 바라보며 말했다.
"우린 따라가야 해."

"따라가다니 무슨 말이야?" 마이크가 긴장한 목소리로 말했다. "그건 벽이야. 그냥 뚫고 갈 수도 없잖아."

"아니," 내가 말했다. "하지만 이건 뭔가로 이어지고 있어. 지난번엔 사물함 근처였고, 지금은 벽 안이야. 우리가 복도를 따라가면... 다시 들을 수 있을지도 몰라."

다들 불안한 표정이었지만, 내가 걷기 시작하자 따라왔다. 우리는 바보처럼 몇 걸음마다 벽에 귀를 대며 천천히 움직였다. 선생님 하나가 우리를 이상하게 쳐다보고 지나갔지만, 아무 말도 하지 않았다.

그때 제임스가 멈춰 섰다.

"얘들아," 그가 속삭였다. "들어 봐."

우리는 귀를 기울였다.

이번엔 더 또렷했다. 단순한 속삭임이 아니었다. 말이었다.

“아래로… 추워… 도와줘…”

목소리는 움직이고 있었다. 아니면 이끌고 있었다. 학교 안 더 깊은 곳으로.

우리는 따라갔다.

과학실 뒤의 긴 복도를 지나고, 관리실을 지나, 체육관 쪽으로.

가까이 갈수록, 공기가 점점 차가워졌다. 그냥 시원한 게 아니었다—축축했다. 오랫동안 햇빛을 보지 못한 지하 공간 같은 냉기였다.

체육관 문에 도착했을 때, 목소리는 멈췄다.

우리는 넷 다, 거칠게 숨을 쉬며 멈춰 섰다. 복도는 죽은 듯 고요했다.

“왜 체육관이지?” 윌이 창백한 얼굴로 물었다.

“몰라,” 내가 말했다. “하지만 여기까지 왔어.”

마이크가 망설였다. “별일 아니겠지. 그냥 오래된 건물에서 나는 소리일 거야.”

"그럼 왜 계속 '도와줘'라고 해?" 내가 물었다.

그는 대답하지 않았다.

제임스가 이중문을 밀었다. 쇠문이 삐걱거리며 경고하듯 소리를 냈다. 체육관 안은 어두웠다—높은 창문 틈 사이로 희미한 빛이 스며들 뿐. 우리는 걸음을 옮겼고, 발걸음 소리가 반짝이는 마룻바닥 위로 울렸다.

이상한 건 보이지 않았다.
관중석은 접혀 있었고, 농구 골대는 가만히 매달려 있었다.
다른 사람은 아무도 없었다.

하지만 뭔가 이상했다.

"이거 싫어," 존이 속삭였다. "누가 우리를 보고 있는 느낌이야."

우리는 마치 벌칙 게임이라도 하듯, 체육관 한가운데로 몰려들었다. 침묵은 너무 무거웠고, 마치 가장자리가 날카로운 칼처럼 느껴졌다.

그때 제임스가 속삭였다.
"저기."

그는 저 멀리 벽 근처의 사각형 윤곽을 가리켰다—함정 문이거나 유지 관리용 덮개 같았다. 멀리서 보면 거의 보이지 않았다. 아무도 전에 본 적이 없었다.

우리는 천천히 다가갔다.

그건 나무 바닥과 평평하게 맞닿은 금속판이었다.

표시는 없었다. 손잡이도 없었다. 단지 희미한 이음선과 네 개의 묵직한 나사들.

"나 이게 있는지도 몰랐어." 내가 말했다.

"나도," 제임스가 말했다. "6학년 때부터 다녔는데 처음 봐."

나는 무릎을 꿇고 먼지를 털어 냈다.

그때, 다시 들렸다.

속삭임이 아니었다.

노크 소리였다.

세 번. 느리게. 바닥 아래에서.

존이 벌떡 뒷걸음쳤다. 눈이 휘둥그레졌다.

"됐어. 난 여기서 나갈래. 이건 미친 짓이야."

"아니야," 내가 말했다. "아직 끝난 게 아니야."

"체육관 밑에 뭔가 있어," 마이크가 떨리는 목소리로 말했다. "정상이 아냐."

"나도 알아. 그래서 지금 멈추면 안 돼."

또 한 번의 노크.

그리고 정적.

우리는 숨조차 쉬지 않고 서 있었다.

"여기 아래엔 뭐가 있는 거지?" 제임스가 마침내 물었다.

"창고?"

"지하실," 내가 말했다. "여기가 막힌 입구인 것 같아."

그들이 나를 바라봤다.

"도서관에서 어떤 분을 만났어," 내가 계속 말했다.
"예전에 이 학교 다녔다고 했어.
이 학교 지하에 수영장이 있었다고...
근데 닫혔다고. 문은 용접됐고.
그리고 한 아이가 거기서 실종됐다고 했어."

"야..." 제임스가 말했다. "장난치지 마."

"장난 아니야."

긴 침묵. 그리고 제임스가 말했다.
"그럼... 이제 뭐 할 건데?"

나는 덮개를 다시 바라보았다.

"방법을 찾아서 들어갈 거야."

아무도 말하지 않았다.

그때 제임스가 한숨을 쉬었다.
"진짜 싫다. 아주 싫어.
근데 널 혼자 보낼 순 없어."

존이 신음했다.

“이래서 영화에서 사람들이 죽는 거야.”

하지만 한 명씩, 모두 고개를 끄덕였다.

두려워도, 남았다.

그리고 그 순간에도,

우리 발아래 어둠 속 어딘가엔...

무언가가 기다리고 있었다.

제 5장

✦

서랍

쿵.

쿵.

쿵.

그 소리는 체육관 바닥 아래에서 심장처럼 울려 퍼졌다—느리고, 꾸준하고, 분명하게.

우리는 그대로 얼어붙었다. 아무도 말하지 않았다. 늘 말이 많던 제임스조차 창백한 얼굴로 침묵했다.

윌이 먼저 속삭였다.

"얘들아... 우리 여기서 나가야 해."

하지만 나는 앞으로 나아갔다. 눈은 바닥에 있던 금속 사각형 윤곽선—그 해치인지 뭔지 모를 것—에 고정되어 있었다. 나는 무릎을 꿇고 손가락으로 틈을 따라 문질렀다.

"손잡이가 없어. 위에서 완전히 봉인됐어," 내가 중얼거렸다.

"좋네," 윌이 말했다. "닫혀 있어야 한다는 뜻이잖아."

제임스가 주위를 둘러보았다. "다른 길이 있을 거야. 이걸 봉인했다면, 다른 입구도 있었을지 몰라. 측면 출입구나 유지 관리실 같은 거?"

그때 나는 갑자기 떠올렸다.

"저장실," 내가 말했다. "체육관 옆에 있는 거. 체육 시간 끝나고 한 번 본 적 있어. 문이 열려 있었는데, 안쪽이 생각보다 깊었어. 어쩌면 지하로도 이어질 수 있어."

마이크가 눈썹을 치켜들었다. "그리고 그게... 수영장으로 이어진다고 생각해?"

“어쩌면. 하지만 확인하지 않으면 모르는 거잖아.”

제임스는 고개를 끄덕이며 이미 걷기 시작했다. “가자.”

윌은 뒤에서 신음했다.
“왜 이런 게 꼭 공포 영화 같지?”

체육관 밖 복도는 조용했다. 너무 조용했다.
우리는 빠르게 움직였다. 소리 내지 않으려 애쓰며 사물함을 지나, ‘장비 보관실 - 관계자 외 출입 금지’라고 적힌 녹슨 문으로 향했다.

나는 손잡이를 잡았다.

잠겨 있었다.

당연히.

혹시나 하는 마음에 흔들어 봤지만, 역시 열리지 않았다.

“끝났네,” 윌은 이미 등을 돌리며 말했다.

하지만 마이크가 앞으로 나섰다.
“잠깐만.”

그는 배낭을 열고 필통을 꺼냈다. 그 안에서 클립 두 개를 꺼내 재빠르게 펴며 손을 고정시켰다.

"튜토리얼 영상 본 적 있어," 그가 무릎을 꿇으며 말했다. "클립으로 자물쇠 따는 거. 한번 해 보고 싶었거든."

윌은 놀라 입을 벌렸다. "뭐? 너 몰래 잠금 해제 배우고 있었어?"

"아무것도 안 하고 서 있는 것보단 낫잖아," 마이크가 중얼거리며 클립 하나를 자물쇠에 넣고, 다른 하나로 조심스럽게 움직였다.

찰칵.

우리는 모두 귀를 기울였다.

찰칵.

제임스가 낮게 휘파람을 불었다.
"이거 열면, 일주일 내내 점심 내가 쏜다."

마이크는 대답하지 않았다. 이마에 주름을 지며 집중했다. 클립을 다시 조정했다.

찰칵.

자물쇠가 부드럽게 풀렸다.

마이크가 웃으며 말했다. "타코 사 줘."

"콜," 제임스가 말했다.

윌은 입을 반쯤 벌린 채 바라보았다. "우리 다 감옥 갈 거야."

나는 자물쇠를 떼고 조심스럽게 문을 열었다.

곰팡이와 금속이 섞인 듯한 냄새가 뿜어져 나왔다. 오래된, 잊힌 공간에만 남아 있는 냄새였다. 안쪽은 어두웠다—천장에 달린 낡은 전등 하나가 윙윙거리며 희미하게 빛났다.

벽에는 오래된 레슬링 매트가 기대어 있었고, 망이 엉킨 채 쌓인 카트와 먼지 덮인 체육 장비들이 선반에 어수선하게 놓여 있었다.

문은 부드럽게 닫히며 딸깍 소리를 냈다.

그 소리가 싫었다.

우리는 함께 안쪽으로 들어갔다.

“여기 분위기 진짜 소름 돋아,” 존이 중얼거렸다. “왜 이렇게 넓은 거야?”

“보관용이지,” 제임스가 핸드폰 불빛을 비추며 말했다. “무서운 비밀들을 위한.”

그리고 우리는 봤다—방 제일 뒤편.

회색 금속 서랍장.
높고, 찌그러졌으며, 몇 번은 걷어차인 듯한 자국.
맨 위 서랍엔 희미하게 적힌 라벨이 있었다:

관리부 – 보관 기록

나는 심장이 두근거리며 앞으로 나아갔다.
맨 위 손잡이를 잡아당기자, 금속이 크르륵 소리를 내며 열렸다.

안에는 서류 더미, 오래된 파일, 라미네이트 된 시간표, 먼지 묻은 출석부가 뒤엉켜 있었다.

“찾아보자,” 내가 말했다.

우리는 빠르게 뒤적였다. 봉투를 열고, 페이지를 넘기며 훑어보았다.

“쓸모 있는 건 없네,” 제임스가 1997년 체육부 예산 폴더를 던지며 말했다.

그러다 두 번째 서랍에서, 헐거운 종이들 사이에 끼어 있는 낡은 신문 스크랩이 눈에 들어왔다.

나는 조심스럽게 꺼냈다.

제목은 희미했지만 읽을 수 있었다.
“웨스트브리지 학생 실종. 수사 진행 중.”

사진도 있었다. 흐릿하고 거칠었다. 우리 또래로 보이는 한 소년. 후드티를 입고, 어두운 눈빛. 사물함 줄 옆에 서 있었다.

가슴이 뻐근해졌다.

기사는 짧았다. 고작 한 단락.
어떻게 실종됐는지는 적혀 있지 않았다.
날짜도 없었다. 단지 한 이름: Evan R.
마지막 목격 장소는 체육관 근처. 그 이후 목격자는 없음.

나는 그것을 들여다보다, 친구들에게 건넸다.

제임스는 읽고 빠르게 넘겼다. 표정은 읽기 어려웠다.

"이게... 끝이야?"

윌은 찡그리며 읽었다. "이게 다야? 한 단락?"

마이크가 마지막으로 받았다. 고개를 저었다.
"경찰 보고서도 없고? 후속 기사도 없고? 그냥... 이게 끝?"

"이게 아무것도 아니라고?" 내가 말했다. "이건 그가 실제로 존재했다는 증거야."

제임스는 목덜미를 문질렀다.
"나는 뭔가 더 큰 걸 기대했어. 비밀 통로라든가, 설계도라든가.
이건 그냥 먼지 묻은 기사 한 장이잖아."

"우린 노크 소리 들었잖아," 내가 날카롭게 말했다. "뭔가 아래에 있다는 거 알잖아."

"그리고 이제는 누군가 거기 있었단 것도 알았지," 마이크가 말했다.
"하지만 죽었다는 증거는 없어. 수영장이랑 관련 있다는 것도."

윌은 팔짱을 꼈다. "그래서 이제 뭐 할 건데? 체육관 바닥 뚫어? 터널

파? 난 빠질래. 이건 더 이상 재미없어."

공기가 무거워졌다. 현실이 다시 우리를 덮치는 것 같았다.

"그냥 가자," 존이 중얼거렸다. "해도 너무 늦었어."

아무도 반박하지 않았다.

우리는 조용히 서랍을 닫고 보관실을 빠져나왔다. 나는 문을 다시 잠그고, 자물쇠를 제자리에 끼웠다.

학교를 나설 때쯤, 해가 지고 있었고, 운동장은 길고 긴 그림자에 잠겨 있었다. 우리는 각자 말없이 집으로 향했다.

나는 집에 도착해 침대에 앉았다. 그리고 그 기사를 다시 펼쳤다.
손가락으로 에반의 이름을 따라 문질렀다.

아무도 이 이야기의 뒷면이 있다고 믿지 않았다.

하지만 나는 알았다.

체육관 아래 어딘가에서...
에반은 아직 기다리고 있었다.

제 6장

✦

비어 있는 자들

수업이 끝난 후 도착했을 때, 도서관은 거의 비어 있었다.

차가운 이슬비가 보도 위를 적시고 있었고, 구름은 낮게 드리워져 회색으로 빛을 가렸다. 나는 후드를 털고 조용함 속으로 걸어 들어갔다. 이곳에 들어올 때마다 느끼는 그 무거운, 누군가가 지켜보는 듯한 고요함이 다시 나를 짓눌렀다.

이번에는 책장 쪽으로 가지 않았다.

곧장 도서관 뒤편의 같은 자리로 향했다. 깜빡이는 전구 아래, 지역 역사 섹션이 먼지 낀 비밀을 간직한 채 자리를 지키고 있었다.

나는 그 익숙한 두꺼운 책—**『웨스트브리지의 역사』**—을 꺼내어 다시 펼쳤다.

136페이지와 137페이지. 여전히 부자연스럽고, 여전히 무언가 잘못 되어 있었다.

그래서 이번엔 다른 것을 찾기 시작했다. 무엇이든.

다른 책들의 색인을 뒤졌다.
시의 인구 조사 기록을 살폈다.
오래된 도시 계획 문서까지 찾아보았다.

분은 시간이 되고, 시간은 흐릿해졌다.
눈이 아팠다. 창밖 빗소리는 점점 희미해져 백색 소음처럼 느껴졌다.

그때, 그녀의 기척이 다시 느껴졌다.

"아직도 파고 있니?"
도서관 여자가 조용히 말했다.

나는 깜짝 놀라 몸을 움찔했다.
그녀는 내 옆에 서 있었고, 손에는 작고 따뜻한 차가 담긴 컵이 들려 있었다. 카디건은 어깨에 느슨하게 걸쳐 있었고, 목소리는 차분했지만, 그녀가 나를 바라보는 방식은—이미 내가 무엇을 찾고 있는지 알고 있다는 걸 말해 주고 있었다.

“알아야 해요,” 내가 말했다. “에반에 대해서. 수영장에 대해서. 노크 소리에 대해서.”

그녀는 천천히 고개를 끄덕였다.

“대부분 아이들은 겁먹고 그만두지. 하지만 넌 대부분 아이들과는 다르구나. 그렇지?”

나는 대답하지 못했다.

그럴 수 없었다.

그녀는 주변을 둘러본 뒤, 살짝 몸을 숙이며 속삭였다.

“이곳엔 사람들이 더 이상 사용하지 않는 방이 하나 있어. 원래 도서관 일부가 아니었어—예전엔 주정부 기록 담당 부서였지. ‘역사 보존국’이라 불렸지만, 실상은 기록 삭제자들이었어.”

“기록 삭제자들이요?” 내가 물었다.

“과거를 지우는 일을 맡은 사람들이지,” 그녀가 담담히 말했다.

“이름을 바꾸고, 파일을 봉인하고, 때로는 불태우기도 했어.”

나는 입이 바짝 말랐다.

“왜 저한테 이걸 말해 주는 거죠?”

그녀는 내 눈을 똑바로 바라보았다.

"나도 그 학교에 다녔거든. 그리고... 네가 준비됐다고 생각해."

그녀는 스웨터 주머니에서 낡은 황동 열쇠 하나를 꺼냈다.

낡은 가죽 태그가 달려 있었다.

Room B12.

"지하에 있어," 그녀가 말했다.

"조용히 가렴. 너무 오래 있진 말고."

나는 떨리는 손으로 열쇠를 받았다.

"감사합니다."

그녀는 희미하게 미소 지었지만, 거기엔 따뜻함이 없었다.

그저 지친 표정뿐이었다.

"한 번 열린 문은... 다시는 완전히 닫히지 않아."

도서관 지하 복도는 건물의 다른 부분보다 오래된 듯한 느낌이었다.

벽은 두껍고, 공기는 차가웠다.

나는 좁은 복도를 따라 걸었고, 결국 칠이 벗겨진 문 하나를 찾았다— Room B12.

번호는 거의 지워져 있었다.

나는 열쇠를 조용히 돌려 문을 열었다.

안은 창 없는 작은 방이었다.
금속 캐비닛, 바인더, 수십 년 전 날짜가 적힌 상자들이 빼곡히 들어차 있었다.
천장에는 전구 하나가 매달려 있었고, 갓 떠난 사람처럼 희미하게 흔들리고 있었다.

나는 선반을 훑었다.
그리고 **Westbridge Middle – Classified Internal Reports(웨스트브리지 중학교 – 내부 기밀 보고서)**라고 적힌 폴더 하나를 발견했다.

안에는 복사된 문서들이 한가득이었다.
수십 페이지.
REDACTED(삭제됨), INTERNAL ONLY(내부용), DO NOT DUPLICATE(복제 금지) 등의 도장이 선명했다.

나는 먼지 쌓인 책상에 앉아 읽기 시작했다.

연례 사건 검토 – 웨스트브리지 중학교 – 내부용

연도: 2005

실종자 수: 6명

나이: 11–13세

사건 유형: 설명되지 않은 실종

공식 발표: 가스 누출 – 대피 조치 – 임시 전학

공식 수사: 없음

최종 상태: 사건 종결

연도: 2006

실종자 수: 6명

공식 발표: 노선 변경 – 가족 이주 공지 사후 발송

최종 상태: 사건 종결

매년. 여섯 명.

다른 변명. 다른 거짓. 하지만 항상 같은 수.

그리고 나는 그것을 보았다.

제목: 집단 형성 – "비어 있는 자들(The Hollow Ones)"

심장이 멎는 듯했다.

비어 있는 자들은 1990년대 후반, 학생들이 자체적으로 만든 집단으로 추정됨.

구성 인원은 최대 6명.

목적은 미상.

사용되지 않는 수영장 시설을 중심으로 한 무허가 야간 활동이 주축으로 여겨짐.

초기 리더는 에반 R.(전체 이름 삭제됨)로 확인됨.

전직 관리인의 증언에 따르면(이름 미공개), 의식적인 도전 과제가 자주 이루어졌으며, 고립, 수중 잠수, 지하 통로 접근이 포함됨.

알려진바, 최소 3명의 구성원이 학기 중 실종되었으며, 일부는 여름 방학 중 사라짐.

지역 당국과 교육 위원회의 협조로 공식 은폐 서사가 유지됨.

외부 보도 금지.

가족에겐 보상 제공.

목격자는 침묵하도록 처리됨.

나는 침을 삼켰다. 손이 떨렸다.

페이지를 넘겼다.

거기엔 도면이 있었다.

수영장 배치도 스케치.

보안 카메라 기록—대부분 검게 칠해져 있거나 “복구 불가”라고 적혀 있었다.

그리고, 손 글씨로 된 메모 하나가 눈에 들어왔다.

“비어 있는 자들은 해산되지 않았다.
리더가 남아 있다면, 문도 남아 있다.
굶주림도 마찬가지다.”

나는 그 자리에 멍하니 앉아 있었다.

이건 단순한 유령 이야기가 아니었다.

어둠 속의 속삭임이 아니었다.

그들은 실재했다.
그리고 누군가—에반—이 그걸 시작했다.

하지만 왜?

아직은 몰랐다.

하지만 분명한 건 하나 있었다.
누군가 수년 동안 이 모든 걸 은폐해 왔다.
학교. 경찰. 어쩌면 그 이상.

가짜 뉴스. 조작된 발표.
진실을 감추기 위한 거짓말.

그리고 아이들은 계속해서 사라졌다.

나는 자리에서 일어났다.
심장은 미친 듯이 뛰었다.

이제 나는 더 이상 무서워하는 게 아니었다.
분노했다.

이 사실을 아는 사람은 이제 나뿐이었다.

그리고 만약 에반이 여전히 남아 있다면,
올해 말까지 또 여섯 명이 사라질 수도 있다.

그건 절대 막아야만 했다.

이제 나는 새로운 목표를 가졌다.

에반을 찾아낸다.
진실을 밝힌다.
그리고 이 모든 걸 끝낸다.

제 7장

✦

네가 다음이야

그날은 평소처럼 시작되었다.

하늘은 유난히 파랗고, 태양은 내가 느끼는 감정과는 다르게 너무 눈부시게 빛났다.

학생들은 복도로 하나둘 흘러 들어와 웃고, 소리치며, 가방을 한쪽 어깨에 걸치고 스쳐 지나갔다.

선생님들은 교실 문 앞에 서서 커피를 홀짝이며 인사를 건넸다.

하지만 나에겐 아무것도 정상처럼 느껴지지 않았다.

Room B12에서 읽은 것들 이후로는.

비어 있는 자들(The Hollow Ones)의 진실을 알게 된 이후로는.

나는 유령처럼 복도를 걸었다.
눈은 그림자, 환풍구, 어둡게 죽은 구석을 훑었다.
에반의 이름이 내 머릿속에서 계속 경고처럼 울려 퍼졌다.

아무도 몰랐다.
하지만 나는 알았다.

그것만으로도 나는 표적이 된 셈이었다.

3교시로 향하던 중, 나는 정신을 가다듬기 위해 화장실로 들어갔다.
형광등은 윙윙거리며 깜빡였고, 공간은 텅 비어 있었다.
내 발소리만이 타일 위에서 메아리쳤다.

나는 수도꼭지를 틀고 찬물을 얼굴에 끼얹었다.
그리고 고개를 들어 거울을 바라봤다.

그 순간, 몸이 얼어붙었다.

거울 위, 김이 서린 유리면에—무언가가 긁혀 있었다.

처음엔 그냥 지저분한 자국처럼 보였다.
하지만 내가 가까이 다가가자 그 글자가 보였다.

"네가 다음이야(YOU'RE NEXT)."

글자는 날카롭고 삐뚤빼뚤했다.
열쇠나 동전 모서리로 긁은 듯했다.

입이 바짝 말랐다.
나는 뒷걸음질을 쳤다. 심장이 요동쳤다.

이건 장난이 아니었다.

내가 아는 걸 아는 사람은 없었다.

누군가가 나를 지켜보고 있었다.

에반(Evan) 같은 누군가가.

나는 화장실을 둘러보았다—아무도 없었다.
칸막이는 비어 있었고, 유일하게 들리는 건 한쪽 싱크대에서 똑... 똑... 떨어지는 물소리뿐이었다.

그때, 속삭임이 다시 들렸다.

말이 아닌, 숨소리.

깨진 타일 사이로 누군가 숨을 내쉬는 것 같은 소리.

나는 가방을 움켜쥐고 그대로 달려 나갔다.

점심시간쯤, 나는 친구들을 식당 구석으로 끌고 갔다.
다른 학생들의 소음은 아주 멀게 느껴졌다.

"봤어," 내가 말했다.
"거울에. 누가 긁어 놨어."

"뭐라고?" 제임스가 피자 한 조각을 씹으며 물었다.

"'네가 다음이야.' 그렇게 적혀 있었어. 거울에. 누군가 내가 파일을 본 걸 안 거야. 날 경고하는 거야."

윌은 곧바로 공포에 질린 표정이 되었다.
"이건… 진짜 끝이야. 그만둬야 해. 우리 전부. 너무 심각해졌어."

"아니," 내가 단호하게 말했다.
"오히려 이게 증거야. 우리가 미친 게 아니라는. 에반은 진짜야. 비어 있는 자들은 진짜야. 그리고 우리가 진실을 본 걸 알고 있어."

마이크가 몸을 앞으로 숙이며 낮은 목소리로 말했다.

"그래서... 이제 뭐 할 거야?"

나는 그들을 바라보았다.
그들의 눈엔 공포가 있었지만, 나와 같은 결심도 있었다.

"의식을 해 보자," 내가 말했다.

제임스는 눈을 깜빡였다.
"진심이야?"

"파일 안에 의식에 대한 부분적인 설명이 있었어.
비어 있는 자들은 그 의식을 밤에, 수영장에서 했다고."

윌이 목소리를 떨며 말했다.
"그런데... 존재하지도 않는 수영장에 어떻게 들어가?"

"침입해야지. 체육관을 통해. 그 해치로. 아니면 다른 입구가 있을 수도 있어."

마이크는 천천히 고개를 끄덕였다.
"만약 에반이 이걸 시작했다면, 우리도 그 방식으로 끝낼 수 있을지도 몰라."

윌은 얼굴을 손으로 감쌌다.

"미쳤어. 진짜."

"어쩌면 그렇지," 내가 말했다.

"하지만 차라리 미친놈이 되는 게 낫지.

다음 차례가 되는 것보단."

종이 울렸다.

우리는 식판과 가방을 챙겼고, 나는 그들을 향해 내가 평생 말할 줄 몰랐던 말을 꺼냈다.

"오늘 밤 자정에 학교에서 만나.

손전등 챙겨.

그리고 용기를 낼 수 있는 어떤 것이라도 가져와."

제임스는 억지로 웃으며 말했다.

"농담도 포함이냐?"

"아니. 오늘 밤은 안 돼."

그날 밤, 나는 손전등, 여분의 배터리, 장갑, 그리고 에반에 대한 신문 기사를 가방에 넣었다.

손은 떨렸지만, 두려움 때문은 아니었다.
기대감 때문이었다.

무언가가 시작되었다.

이제 되돌릴 수 없었다.

내일 아침이 오면, 모든 것이 달라질 것이다.

좋든 나쁘든.

제 8장

✦

수영장

학교는 내가 본 어느 때보다 어두웠다.

자정이 되자 복도는 더 이상 단순한 복도가 아니었다—그것은 그림자의 터널이었고, 사방에 늘어선 사물함들은 마치 침묵하는 파수꾼처럼 보였다.

우리는 손전등을 켜고 함께 천천히, 한 걸음씩 앞으로 나아갔다.

"왜 이렇게 학교가 우릴 보고 있는 것 같지?" 윌이 속삭이며 주위를 둘러보았다.

"아마 진짜로 보고 있나 보지," 제임스가 떨리는 웃음으로 말했다. 하지만 그의 목소리는 중간에 갈라졌다. "걱정 마. 유령이 나타나면... 음,

농담이라도 해 줄게."

"유령은 웃지 않아," 마이크가 중얼대며 체육관 문을 밀었다.

존은 마지막으로 따라왔다. 그는 문턱에 멈춰서 손전등을 체육관 안으로 비췄다.

"이건 진짜 나쁜 생각이야." 그가 조용히 말했다.

"나도 같이하기로 했지만... 뭔가 잘못됐어."

"지금이라도 돌아가도 돼." 내가 말했다.

그는 나와 다른 애들을 번갈아 보았다.

"너희만 두고 가긴 싫어. 근데 무언가 튀어나오면, 나 진짜 비명 지를 거야."

체육관은 정적에 휩싸여 있었다. 나무 바닥은 손전등 불빛에 희미하게 반짝였다.

우리는 체육관 중앙쯤에 멈췄고, 바닥에 희미하게 보이는 사각형 윤곽선이 눈에 들어왔다.

"저기야." 내가 가리키며 말했다.

"그래, 아직도 잠겨 있네." 윌이 말했다. "우리가 이걸 어쩌겠—"

그가 말을 끝마치기도 전에 마이크가 무릎을 꿇고 주머니에서 종이 클립 두 개를 꺼냈다.
"내가 빈손으로 올 줄 알았어? 이번엔 자물쇠 따는 영상 두 개 더 봤거든."

제임스가 비웃었다. "좋아. 오늘 우리가 죽는다면, 널 탓하면 되겠네."

"왜 자물쇠를 얘한테 맡긴 거지?" 존이 한쪽 눈썹을 치켜올렸다.

"왜냐하면," 마이크가 말하며 자물쇠에 클립을 끼워 넣었다.
"여기서 종이 클립이랑 유튜브 프리미엄 있는 사람은 나뿐이거든."

찰칵.

하나의 볼트가 풀렸다.

우리는 모두 숨을 죽이고 몸을 기울였다.
공기 중의 긴장감은 어둠보다 더 두껍게 느껴졌다.

찰칵. 쾅!

마지막 볼트가 열렸다.

해치가 삐걱거리며 들렸다.

안에서 공기가 새어 나왔다—차갑고 축축하며, 희미하게 염소 냄새와 녹슨 쇠 내음이 섞여 있었다.

"세상에…" 제임스가 속삭였다. "진짜 있었어."

윌은 한발 물러섰다.
"얘들아. 아니야. 진짜 이건 공포 영화에서 사람 죽는 타이밍이야."

"이제 돌아갈 수 없어," 내가 말했다. "에반이 저 아래에 있다면, 지금이 기회야."

마이크는 가방끈을 조였다.
"넌 혼자 안 가."

나는 모두를 바라보았다—제임스, 마이크, 윌, 존.

존은 천천히 숨을 내쉬었다.
"이건 평생 트라우마가 될 거야, 그렇지?"

"직접 확인해 보자," 내가 말했다.

우리는 내려갔다.

계단은 가파르고 좁았고, 양옆 벽은 차가웠다.
한 걸음 내디딜 때마다 금속 소리가 울렸다.
아래로 내려갈수록 공기는 점점 더 차가워지고, 습기로 무거워졌다.
마침내 도착했을 때, 앞에는 금속 문 하나가 살짝 열려 있었다.

제임스가 두 손가락으로 문을 밀었다.
"이거 문 닫히면... 나 유령 상대로 소송할 거야."

나는 숨을 참으며 안으로 들어섰다.

그리고 그곳에 그게 있었다.

수영장.

고요하고, 맑고, 믿기지 않게 깨끗한 물.
천장에서 깜빡이는 불빛 아래에서 연하게 빛나고 있었다.
수년 동안 방치됐을 공간인데, 거짓말처럼 아름다웠다—그것도 섬뜩한 방식으로.

"여기... 진짜라면 역겨워야 맞는 거 아니냐?" 마이크가 말했다. "막 진흙, 쥐, 악취 뭐 그런 걸로."

"응," 존이 중얼거렸다. "근데 이건 그냥... 지옥에서 온 스파 같다."

윌은 그저 멍하니 바라봤다. 얼굴이 하얗게 질렸다.
"싫어. 이거 뭔가 이상해. 자연스럽지 않아."

"맞아," 내가 말했다. "하지만 진짜야."

우리는 수영장 가장자리로 모였다.
바닥 타일은 얼음처럼 차가웠다.
나는 재킷 주머니에서 손으로 쓴 의식 노트를 꺼내 조심스럽게 펼쳤다.

"원을 만들어야 해," 내가 말했다. "손을 잡고. 이 말을 따라 해."

"진짜야?" 존이 눈을 치켜떴다. "우리가 이걸 진짜 한다고?"

"응."

마이크가 고개를 끄덕였다.
"빨리 끝내자."

제임스가 한숨 쉬었다.
"보자. 만약 물귀신한테 잡아먹히면, 누가 우리 엄마한테 내가 초자연적 미스터리 풀다 죽었다고 전해 줘."

우리는 하나씩 물 안으로 들어갔다.
차가운 물이 전기처럼 퍼졌다—맑고, 날카롭고, 즉각적이었다.
허리까지 물이 차오를 때까지 걸어 들어갔다.
숨결이 하얗게 피어올랐다.

우리는 손을 잡았다.
원이 완성됐다.

"다들 괜찮지?" 내가 물었다.

윌은 울 것 같은 얼굴이었다.
"'괜찮다'의 정의부터 다시 하자."

"나 여기 있어," 존이 조용히 말했다.
"끝내자."

우리는 모두 눈을 감았다.

나는 숨을 들이쉬고 시작했다.

"남아 있는 자여, 우리가 부른다."

다른 애들이 따라 말했다.

"보는 자여, 우리가 부른다."

또다시.

"기다리는 자여, 우리가 부른다."

우리의 목소리가 타일 벽에 울려 퍼졌다.

그리고 침묵.

물이 멈췄다. 공기가 무거워졌다.
우리는 그 자리에 그대로 서서, 떨며 기다렸다.

"이제 뭐?" 제임스가 속삭였다.

"나도 모—"

그 순간, 물이 움직였다.

우리 때문이 아니었다.

무언가가 아래에서 움직였다.

"방금 느꼈지?" 윌이 속삭였다. 손을 꽉 쥐었다.

"응," 존이 숨죽이며 말했다. "우리가 아니었어."

그리고 소리가 들렸다.

목소리.

깊은 곳에서. 희미하게.

"...왜 나를 불렀지?"

우리는 모두 얼어붙었다.

"얘들아." 제임스의 목소리가 떨렸다. "방금 그거... 우리 중 누구도 아니었지?"

"원을 깨지 마," 내가 단호하게 말했다. "무슨 일이 있어도—절대 떨어지지 마."

그리고 수면 아래에서, 무언가가 올라오기 시작했다.

제 9장

✦

밧줄

문이 한숨을 쉬듯 열렸다. 마치 세상이 스스로 숨을 내쉬는 것처럼.

문 너머엔 어둠이 아니었다—정확히 말하면.

현실보다 얇은 무언가, 마치 간신히 꿰매어진 꿈처럼 흐릿한 공간이었다.

우리는 나란히 그 안으로 걸어 들어갔다. 다섯 명 모두 함께.

그 안의 공간은 회색이고, 흐릿하게 움직였다.

바닥은 단단하지 않았고—발아래 안개처럼 출렁였지만 우리는 떨어지지 않았다.

형체들이 깜빡이며 나타났다 사라졌다.

벽이 생겼다가 녹았고, 책상, 복도, 가로등이 생겼다 이내 사라졌다.

모두 김 서린 유리처럼 증발하는 기억이었다.

“이건 현실이 아니야,” 마이크가 속삭였다.

“아니,” 내가 말했다. “이건 기억이야.”

그때, 우리 앞 공중에 밧줄 하나가 떠 있었다.

두껍고, 헤지고, 안개 속으로 끝없이 이어지며 허공에 매달려 있었다.

우리는 밧줄을 따라갔다.

걸음을 옮길 때마다, 기억이 선명해졌다.

점심시간—혼자 앉아 고개를 숙이고, 음식은 손도 대지 않은 한 소년.
에반.

쉬는 시간—낡은 참나무 아래 혼자 앉은 그.
근처에 아이들이 웃고 있었지만, 그를 보진 않았다.
존재하지 않는 사람처럼.

“난 재를 본 기억이 없어,” 윌이 속삭였다.

"우린 다 그랬어," 존이 조용히 대답했다.

우리는 더 걸었다. 더 많은 기억들이 피어났다.

조용하고 따뜻한 부엌. 엄마가 웃고 있었다.

그러다 병실. 기계 소리.
점점 사라져 가는 아버지.

또 한 걸음.

잠긴 문 앞에 쪼그려 앉아, 액자 속 사진을 품에 안고, 조용히 떨고 있는 에반.

제임스가 낮게 중얼거렸다.
"그는... 모든 걸 잃었어."

밧줄은 계속 이어졌다.

우리는 점점 더 깊이 들어갔다.
에반의 삶, 그의 침묵, 외로움, 세상이 그를 투명 인간처럼 대하던 기억들.

그리고 우리는 그 모습을 보았다.

밧줄의 끝에 서 있던 실루엣.

에반.

뉴스에서 봤던 모습 그대로였다.
후드 티. 그림자 같은 눈.
하지만 여기 있는 그는 귀신도, 괴물도 아니었다.

그저 한 명의 소년.

그는 움직이지 않았다.
우리를 가만히 바라보았다.

그리고 입을 열었다.

너무나 조용히—우리에게 가까스로 닿을 만큼.

"내가 사라지기 전까진, 아무도 나를 보지 않았어."

밧줄은 그의 발아래, 올가미처럼 말려 있었다.

그는 아래를 보고, 다시 우리를 올려다봤다.
그의 표정엔 분노가 아닌, 공허함만이 있었다.

"그냥... 어울리고 싶었어."

그리고 그 순간, 그는 연기처럼 사라졌다.

쾅.

우리 뒤에서 클릭 소리가 울렸다.

우리는 돌아보았다.

기억의 벽에 문 하나가 나타나 있었다.
단순한 하얀 문. 은은히 빛나고 있었다.

나는 친구들을 바라봤다.

아무도 말을 하지 않았다.

우리는 함께 문을 통과했다.

빛.

차가운 공기.

그리고—

삐-삐-삐-삐.

알람 소리.

눈이 번쩍 뜨였다.

햇살이 내 방 창문을 통해 쏟아져 들어왔다.
시계엔 7:00 AM이 깜빡이고 있었다.

가슴이 미친 듯이 뛰었다.

이불은 엉켜 있었고, 옷은 여전히 수영장 물에 젖어 있었다.

나는 자리에서 일어나며 숨을 삼켰다.
현실과 그곳 사이, 어딘가에 끼인 느낌이었다.

이게… 꿈이었을까?

아니면 우리는 진짜 무언가를 지나온 걸까… 그리고 변해 버린 채 돌아온 걸까?

아직은 알 수 없었다.

하지만 곧 알게 될 것이었다.

제 10장

✦

그날 아침 이후

햇빛은 몇 주 만에 가장 따뜻하게 느껴졌다.

나는 집 앞 계단에 앉아 손에 쥔 주스 컵을 바라보며 세상을 지켜보고 있었다.

새들이 지저귀고, 거리 끝에서 개가 짖고, 누군가의 잔디밭에 스프링클러가 느릿하게 돌아가고 있었다.

모든 게 평소처럼 정상이었다.

하지만 나는 내가 정상인지 확신할 수 없었다.

학교는 언제나처럼 흘러갔다.

사물함이 쾅쾅 닫히고, 선생님이 말하고, 친구들이 웃고.
변한 건 없어 보였다.

하지만 분명, 변해 있었다.

수학 시간에 제임스가 팔꿈치로 나를 툭 쳤다.
"저기... 우리, 그거... 꿈이었을까?"

"모르겠어," 내가 대답했다.

마이크가 반대편에서 몸을 기울이며 말했다.
"오늘 아침에도 신발이 여전히 젖어 있었어."

윌도 점심시간에 덧붙였다.
"기억 속에서 내가 그렸던 마커 펜, 아직 주머니에 있어."

존은 아무 말도 하지 않았다.
하지만 그는 식탁 너머로 나를 바라보며 눈빛으로 말했다.
우리 모두 기억하고 있어. 우리가 거기 있었어.

그 후로 우리는 그 일에 대해 많이 말하지 않았다.

말할 필요가 없었기 때문이었다.

그 주말, 나는 혼자 다시 체육관으로 향했다.

확인하고 싶어서.

바닥은 완전히 매끈했다.
틈 하나 없이 이어져 있었고, 해치의 흔적도 없었다.

존재했던 적조차 없는 것처럼.

나는 농구 코트의 중앙에 서서 잠시 가만히 있었다.
귀를 기울였다.
그러나 속삭임도, 두드림도 없었다.

오직 오래된 조명등의 윙윙거리는 소리만이 있었다.

아마 에반은 놓아준 걸지도 몰랐다.

아마 우리는 그를 도와준 걸지도.

아니면, 단지 문이 닫힌 것일 수도 있었다—당분간은.

그날 밤, 나는 서랍 속에 있던 캐러멜의 오래된 사진을 꺼내 침대 머리맡에 놓았다.

눈물은 나오지 않았다.
그저 바라보았다.

세상은 때때로 무언가를 우리에게서 데려가지만, 완전히 떠나는 건 아니다.

기억은 남는다.

그리고 가끔은 우리도, 그 기억에 남는다.

일주일 뒤, 제임스가 단체 채팅방에 메시지를 보냈다.

제임스 누구든 “우리 다시 가 보자” 같은 말 하면 바로 차단함
마이크 진정해. 우린 현실을 구했어. 이제 은퇴임
윌 다신 교실에 칼 들고 오지 마 ㅋㅋ
존 난 아직도 그 밧줄 생각나
나 나는 가끔... 그 문을 봐.
나 꿈속에서.
나 하지만 열진 않아.

잠시 동안 아무도 대답하지 않았다.

그러다 제임스가 마지막 메시지를 보냈다:

제임스 good.

그리고 그걸로 충분했다.

The Hollow Ones

1판 1쇄 발행 2025년 12월 15일
지은이 박태성

교정 주현강 **편집** 이승빈 **마케팅·지원** 이창민
펴낸곳 (주)하움출판사 **펴낸이** 문현광

이메일 haum1000@naver.com **홈페이지** haum.kr
블로그 blog.naver.com/haum1000 **인스타** @haum1007

ISBN 979-11-7374-252-1(43810)

좋은 책을 만들겠습니다.
하움출판사는 독자 여러분의 의견에 항상 귀 기울이고 있습니다.
파본은 구입처에서 교환해 드립니다.